Ganjbaran

Ganjbaran

Or a Persian's Indian Dream

Anahita Kashmirian

ISBN-13: 9781546874058
ISBN-10: 1546874054

اگرفردوس بر روی زمین است،
همین است و همین است و همین است.

امیر خسرو دهلوی

**If there be paradise on earth,
it is this, it is this, it is this.**

Amir Khusrau Dehlavi

The Fable of Two Maharajas

Upon leaving Iran, Sima had no specific destination in mind. She was only intending to stop over in India on her way to an East Asian or Pacific resort, when the name of a palace altered her uncertain plans.

While gazing at her tea cup in the lobby of a hotel in Bombay, she overheard two turbaned maharajas incessantly repeating the word *Ganjbaran*. Their discussion had caught Sima's attention; after all, the two princes were pronouncing a word which in her own native language meant *Abounding with Treasures*. Any Persian speaker would have been intrigued. The maharajas were too absorbed in their conversation to realise that Sima had been overhearing them. It was as if they were recounting fairy tales to each other, but the places they were mentioning appeared so real, and yet out of the ordinary. They were referring to terraced gardens where antelopes leaped like winged fairies from one hill to another, and streams translucent like jewels shimmered between pastures and highland woods.

Sima was mesmerised by the description. The only way she could find out whether *Ganjbaran* actually existed was to interrupt the two princes, and ask them where this fabled palace could be found. From then, each word pronounced by the maharajas worked like a charm. At the end of the conversation, the exiled woman was obsessed with the idea of owning that palace. Spellbound, Sima inquired after the owner of the property, and not long afterwards she was admiring its gates. The palace enticed her from the first glance.

THE CELESTIAL LAND

Constructed on a hill, the palace was conspicuous from miles away, appearing like a sanctuary. The magnificent entrance was no less impressive than the residence itself: the gate was composed of a metal door attached to two colossal pillars at whose base were two marble statues of formidable mythical birds, which might have been a phoenix or a *simurgh*. From there a stone passageway led to the palace, in front of which was a broad terrace with seven broad purple pillars. Majestic stairways flanked the terrace on either side.

The walls and the roof were painted in blue, whereas all the protruding parts of the building were tinted in purple. The domes, the statues of gods standing in the niches of the wall, the reliefs, the mural sculptures, and all the engravings were conspicuous due to the sharp contrast between the faded purple and the blue.

A long waterway flowed from the front terrace into the garden arranged in four plots, so familiar to Sima, as this was the *Chahrbagh* style she had known in her native Iran. Geometric flower beds covered the landscape. The garden was terraced on multiple layers like a ziggurat. Just before the stairways lay a square basin adorned with floating lotuses and a rising fountain.

The interior of the palace was covered by other masterpieces. Once passed through the vaulted entrances of the building, one could admire the intricate flower patterns on the tiles that covered the lower part of the wall. From the main entrance a corridor led to a large domed hall that had served in bygone days as a lobby. A stained-glass ceiling floated almost seamlessly, stretching across the span of the dome, so that the unending hall was always lit during the day by the brilliant rays of the sun. A rectangular fountained pool occupied the centre of the hall. The position of the room allowed air to pour in freely from the garden and carry along sweet floral aromas. All the rooms opening onto the courtyards were imbued with the scent of roses, while roses which stood like armies dominated the palace's immediate surroundings.

The palace was located in a wooded land in Kashmir considered holy since ancient times. The forest covering the area was called *Drung* by the locals after an old temple which dominated one flank of the woods and was famed for housing an extraordinary well containing water with healing properties. *Ganjbaran* was located in the heart of the *Drung* woods near the temple. The palace used to be the residence of the high priests of the holy site.

Nearby villagers recounted that the palace dated far back to the Vedic period, and was built by the gods. It was a monument whose architecture attested pre-Mogul features. In the fifteenth century the priests left the area and Muslim princes were drawn in by the beauty of the forest and its surrounding monuments. They took ownership of the palace and baptised it *Ganjbaran*. The local people said that once the princes took residence in the palace, for inexplicable motives, they abandoned their father's religion to worship the gods of the local temple, and one by one disappeared mysteriously. During the rule of the British Raj, for some peculiar reason *Ganjbaran* was unoccupied. Its gates remained sealed until the early days of Independence when an abstruse well-to-do family from Qandahar negotiated its purchase from the Maharaja of Kashmir. Since Indian law prohibited Afghans and Iranians from owing property in India, the Qandahari family was soon expropriated and thereafter the palace changed hands between many random well-to-dos. None lasted long on the precincts of *Ganjbaran*, all deciding to evacuate the palace within few months of purchase.

Sima was oblivious to all this history. She stood astounded amid all this beauty, and regarded *Ganjbaran* as a gem. If paradise did exist, this was it. Marvels of this kind, she believed, were non-existent on the other side of the Bosphorus. India was a land of wonders and, above all, a friendly soil. As far as history records, India had always been a land of refuge to Iranians. As a Persian of Indian descent, Sima could relate even more to India. Undoubtedly, it would have been unwise to choose an inhospitable land over the land of the Vedas.

Prior to seeing *Ganjbaran*, a single memory of her home filled her soul with emotion. Objects and buildings which in the past she had taken for granted, had acquired another significance for her. Whilst still in Iran, she had not sensed the value of her ancestral house nor had she appreciated the beauty of the Ecbatani bowls from which her mother drank water - Sima considered them too ordinary. Whilst travelling between countries, she would have given anything to see her old house once more. But as soon as she was struck by the charm of the Kashmiri domain, Sima's state of mind changed. *Ganjbaran* had made her decide that the past offered memories to appreciate the present, and the present provided the opportunity to build joyful memories for the future. The palace became hers.

A FAMILY FROM ELSEWHERE

On her mother's side, Sima had a Russian grandmother: a very melancholic woman who had lived only in the past. She was such an introvert that many wondered how she had found a husband. She too had been exiled. Her family had fallen in disgrace with the Russian court and been forced to leave Russia at the beginning of the century.

The situation was more complicated on her father's side. Her father, Aram Gilipour, had an uncommon accent when he spoke Persian and all the acquaintances and neighbours wondered where he came from. Sima and her immediate family had difficulty admitting before the West-worshipping people of Iran that her father was Indian; however, his dark complexion betrayed non-European origins. Nonetheless, Sima and her family recounted confidently that her father was European. They generally relished misleading people, especially when it came down to their family background and their education.

Sima's father used to travel frequently, and in fact returned very often to his native town in the subcontinent and visited his relatives in India. Sima's mother, Iran Khanum, never accompanied him on his trips. Spiteful gossips recounted that she was having an affair with their young handsome gardener and that two of her five children were actually his as they shared his fair skin and green eyes. Thankfully for all, these rumours never reached her father's ears.

Sima was the youngest child of her family. She and her eldest sister Atoossa definitely were fruit of the legitimate union. Both had dark complexions like their father and beautiful long and straight black hair. A remarkable beauty spot above the mouth distinguished Sima from most other women. With her impeccable white teeth, she resembled the ubiquitous healthy women on Indian toothpaste ads.

Sima had two brothers, Farshid and Jamshid, with whom she had never been on good terms. Both revelled in exercising their power obsessively. As Atoossa and Jima, another sister, were older than them, the brothers' only victim was Sima. Out of grudge, Sima sometimes dropped anonymous notes in her brothers' schoolbags, calling them green-eyed bastards and sons of a boor. Sima operated so skilfully that the brothers never suspected her, and both got into fight with their own classmates, believing some of them to be the culprits.

Jima, the second daughter in the family, was quite a character. The sensible ones in the family usually avoided her as they considered her to be crazy yet nonetheless shrewd. The insightful people of the family alleged that Jima used folly as a cover in order to fool people and take advantage of them. Atoossa was the most sound and serene person of Sima's immediate family. She was the only one trusted and respected inside and outside the Gilipour clan.

AN ENCUMBERING GUEST

Fatally, Sima's days in India were not meant to be spent in serenity. After the Iranian revolution, Jima had no place to go outside Iran. As soon as she heard about Sima's settlement in India, she shamelessly invited herself to Sima's palace. Sima, who was busy decorating her new home, was utterly annoyed by this news. Jima was nothing but a burden, adding hundreds of problems to those she had already. Sima knew that Jima was only good at one thing and that was showing off, despite the fact that she had not achieved much in her life: she had not attended university, and financially she was broke, but this did not prevent her from boasting about both her education and her wealth, completely oblivious to how her ostentatious lies appeared to others.

Sima resigned herself to accept the situation. She had no other choice, as it would have been against the oriental family code to refuse her sister shelter. Sima meditated an hour on the matter and then reflected that, surely in a palace as spacious as hers, Jima wouldn't become an encumbrance. Moreover, her presence would prevent her from feeling lonely. After all, she was in exile, away from all her friends and other relatives. Sima concluded that she should not worry about Jima's sojourn at *Ganjbaran* until the day she had become unbearable.

The following day, Jima's arrival was announced by an old Mercedes that drove into Sima's property honking. Jima refused to descend from the car until the driver opened the door, held her hand and aided her out of the vehicle. She was dressed like an early twentieth-century Russian princess and walked in an affected way, as though she were the Tzarina. Sima came down the stairs to greet her sister, and called one of her servants to carry her sister's baggage and another to serve tea and *ladoos* immediately, as her sister had travelled a long way.

While the two sisters were drinking tea, the big clock in the tearoom struck noon.

"*Would you like to have lunch?*" Sima asked Jima.

With her odd voice, which resembled a rooster's dissonant droning, Jima replied:

"*I am so exhausted that my stomach has stopped sending messages to my brain. It has taken me thirty hours to get from my home to yours. From the onset, my trip was turbulent. On my way to the airport, there was such a congestion due to the Guardians of the Revolution's compulsion to stop every fancy car between the Shah's memorial square and the airport. It took me three hours to reach the airport. The taxi driver wanted to charge me sixty tomans whereas we had agreed on twenty when he picked me up. As you know my dear sister money isn't important to me, but it's the principle. I refused to give into his greed. The driver tagged me as a monarchist and threatened to call the Guardians of the Revolution. I ignored him and shouted for a porter from the open window. The taxi driver thought I was yelling for help. Since no one had ever heard such an elegant lady shout with authority, all eyes were turned to us. The driver jumped out of his car, opened the trunk and handed the porter my luggage. He accepted his twenty tomans and dashed away.*

At the terminal, I had another adventure. The security officer couldn't find my passport. I had applied for my exit visa well in advance, but the officer was arguing that I was blacklisted and that my papers were probably withheld at the passport office. Since I had not told anyone about my plans to leave, I was certain that nobody had filed any false complaints with the officials. I insisted that the man would check his boxes once again. My dear sister, perseverance always helps. The unhappy officer found my passport, but did not want to let go of it. He asked me whether I was related to the royal family. I told him that I felt insulted by his question as there was nothing royal about the family in question. If my aristrocratic demeanor was causing me trouble, my wit saved the day. The man let me go."

Sima, who was getting hungry, took advantage of her sister's pause to get up from the sofa:

"*Jima, you should be ushered to your bedroom right away after such a stressful trip.*"

Jima did not allow her sister to continue:

"Indeed, even though I travelled in first class from Tehran, I was still not comfortable on the plane. The seats were defective. If it were not for you, I wouldn't have gone through the trouble of travelling so far. You don't know how lucky you are that I decided to come to your place. I could have gone to Europe like most of our acquaintances. My daughter Mona has been looking for a house for me in London near Buckingham Palace, but I told her that my youngest sister is all alone in a foreign country with no support. How could I ever go anywhere else without suffering a guilty conscious? I knew that you would need someone with my expertise to run this huge property."

As usual, Jima was being deceptive. Hiding the truth was a sort of habit in the family, and somehow believed to be essential. A lot of energy and hard work is needed to achieve something, whereas to invent a lie about personal wealth and achievement only required a nerve. And there was no shortage of that in the Gilipour household. Most of the lies were told in the fields of education and wealth. It was a sort of hereditary pass-time in the family to brag, and Jima had excelled in that respect. The older she grew, the less capable she became of learning anything intellectually, physically or manually, but the more skilled she became in formulating lies. Even though her education was scarce, she insisted on being recognised as a member of the intelligentsia.

Sima, who was far from being duped from Jima's fibs – being after all, an expert in the subject herself - decided to put an end to her sister's flaunting by asking her if she had brought any caviar from Iran. The Caspian delicacy was not expensive in Iran as it was elsewhere in the world, but Sima knew that her sister did not like spending any money on other people. Jima stammered in such a way that she could not be distinguished from a distraught rooster. She remembered that she had come to her sister's place with empty hands and fell silent.

To strangers, Jima's voice was indeed amusing; however, Sima, like her other siblings, found her sister's voice rather annoying. The silence appeared as a blessing to her, but she felt a bit guilty towards Jima. She decided to assume her responsibilities as a hostess and attend to her sister's needs - to do it otherwise would have been contrary to the Iranian tradition of hospitality. She asked her housekeeper, Chetra, to bring them a small snack. Then Sima adopted a maternal tone, and turned to Jima:

"I have asked Chetra to prepare a special room for you. She is a very caring housekeeper, and I am sure she will attend to all your needs."

Sima then called Chetra again. Chetra arrived immediately:

"Jee Madam."

"Chetra, please show my sister her room."

"Of course, Madam."

Jima was delighted by the idea of taking a nap, and as soon as she was shown to her room she slammed the door in Chetra's face. She did not thank her, as Jima believed servants did not deserve any respect.

Seeking Better Company

In a room set up like an office, Sima sat behind a large old desk imported from Britain during the colonial period. Her gaze was fixed on the window but her thoughts were all focused on Jima. She felt pity for her sister, for Jima had been disturbed by her child's death thirty-six years earlier.

Jima, although capable of being arrogant and difficult, was in fact of a very sensitive nature and had never recovered from her child's death. Her first daughter had been bitten by a scorpion while collecting saffron near the little town of Kashan. Jima who was busy at the time bragging to some of her acquaintances, never forgave herself for neglecting her child in the saffron field.

After the terrible accident her sisters said that she had become odd and eccentric. However, distant relatives and friends said that eccentricities were a common feature in the family and that Jima's insanity did not stem from her daughter's death, but was hereditary. Jima had consulted dozens of doctors and psychiatrists, but her condition had not improved.

Her husband passed away two years after their daughter's death. Gossip had it that Jima's mental condition had killed him, as the poor man had no other means to escape from Jima except leaving this world. The family's version of the drama was that Jima's husband, afflicted by his daughter's loss, had died in sorrow.

Jima did not get along with her second daughter, Mona. The eldest daughter was said to have been very beautiful, but Mona was considered plain. She had a pale-wheat complexion, and a long nose with a big mole beside her left nostril. Unlike most Iranian women, here eyes were dull and inexpressive.

Sima thought again about the size of her palace. Jima's arrival had made her realize that she had not come to India to meditate, and live the life of a

11

hermit. Rather, Sima had come to India to escape aggression and humiliation, to be free to be Iranian, to be free to worship any god or all the gods she wished - a freedom she could not find anywhere else in the world. Sima could not build her nest without any friends and family in the landscape. All her life she had lived among sisters, uncles, aunts and cousins - even at work she had been surrounded by family members. Solitude was unfamiliar to her. She decided to invite Mona to come to India. She wanted to reconcile Mona with her mother. Sima also surmised that with Mona and her children there, Jima would be less of a burden. The other family members would remind her to not take Jima too seriously and laugh at her ramblings from time to time. Jima's arrival had in fact rekindled Sima's sense of kinship.

As Chetra entered Sima's study room, Sima gave her a note on which she had scribbled a telephone number for her to dial. Sima still had no telephone in her office. There was so much refurbishing and repairing to be done that she had decided to postpone the rest of the palace's renovation for another month. Sima walked towards a small enclosure in the main hall of her palace, where Chetra was still on the line talking to an operator. As soon as Chetra stopped talking, Sima took the receiver from her and waited to be connected to London. On the other side of the world, Mona picked up the phone. Sima greeted Mona affectionately:

"Sweet little Mona, how are you?- - How are your children?- - And Karl your husband? -- I would love to meet your family one day. Listen, I have not had the chance to give you a wedding present. Could I make up for it by offering you and your family return tickets to visit me in India?"

In the usual ceremonial Iranian tradition, Sima was at pains to convince Mona that her offer was indeed genuine, and not just a seemingly generous yet vacuous gesture. She said:

"You know Mona that there is no tarof¹ between us. Your mother is in India as well."

Sima was keen to get Mona to accept, and after a few exchanges of news, she gently pressed Mona to confirm that she would be taking up her offer when suddenly their line was disconnected.

---

1 Persian ceremonial tradition of offering presents, food and hospitality. The tone of the person should indicate whether it is sincere or insincere.

Today's Exile, Yesterday's Entrepreneur

Sima had asked Chetra to find her additional help in the nearby village, and the domestic had obliged her mistress by fetching two men and two women one day before Jima's arrival. The two male servants' first task was to prepare the rooms which were adjacent to the golden domed hall. The palace was so wide that in order to keep track of the rooms, successive owners had named each of the halls and wings of the palace. Sima had been given a comprehensive map of *Ganjbaran* listing the function of the various rooms. As the palace needed major repairs, it was not always easy to distinguish, for instance, a study from a music room, or a drawing room from a tea room. Only the reception and ball room were evident owing to their size. More peculiar was the number of kitchens - the palace had three.

Ganjbaran was not Sima's only asset. Prior to the revolution, Sima had acquired many properties in Iran and thus she had become the subject of much gossip. Some said she had been involved in illegal business and that she had acted dishonestly in many financial transactions. Others said that she had slept with a number of billionaires in order to achieve her financial goals. While there was an element of truth in some rumours, much to the dismay of her foes, Sima had never infringed the law - she had plenty of wits and a natural flair for money and lucrative businesses. Sima had begun her career as an administrator in a soap factory, where she dealt with people from all walks of life. However, she was far too ambitious to remain a modest employee, and used all her skills to be promoted. Her boldness allowed her to establish relations with influential people, and very soon enough she became the owner of the soap factory, which she cleverly turned into a huge enterprise that traded internationally. By that time, however, Sima could foresee the impending collapse of the Iranian economy, and she swiftly sold her shares and left Revolutionary Iran with all her wealth, lest she become the victim of the resentful rankers who had suddenly usurped the power.

The Revolution of 1979 had disoriented Sima, but she was determined to remain active. She felt the need to create some distance between herself and the dramatic events that ensued in her country, so she decided to travel for a while. As an Iranian, however, she was no longer welcome in the West. The media had portrayed Iranians as fanatical lunatics, and the average European or American could not distinguish between an Ayatollah from Qum and an Armenian baker from Isfahan. India seemed to her the best choice. Historically, India had accepted all races and religions. From the moment Sima had set foot in Bombay, she felt as a guest of honour. And she wanted to prove that she was worth the honour. In Iran she had not hesitated to help the needy and to set up charitable foundations for building schools and hospitals. Now, she had made it her priority to assist refugees living in India. There were already so many of them from Afghanistan, and an increasing number arriving from Iran in the wake of the Iraqi invasion. Some clerics had offered assurances that those who perished in the war against Iraq's rulers and their Anglo-American allies would be received in heaven. Sima reflected with irony how many young Iranians seemed to prefer a miserable life in the streets of Bombay to that heaven.

The Undesired Guest of an Undesirable Guest

Upstairs in the bedroom, Jima was not able to sleep for long. Sima's garden was full of colourful and exotic birds whose cacophony disturbed Jima's sleep. It took a long time before Jima could properly open her eyes. She was drowsy due to the sleeping pills she had taken the previous night, and she felt lonely. She was comforted by the thought that her sister was downstairs, but still felt nostalgic about her days in Iran. Since Iranians were hospitable, she had always had somewhere to go. This did not prevent her from infringing the Iranian code of hospitality when she avoided hosting guests at her own residence. Jima's motto was: '*As long as I am enjoying myself, to hell with the others.*' Only on rare occasions did Jima have people round for tea, and even then they were required to have an appointment - extremely un-Iranian.

Jima had a pretentious personality in need of an audience, hence her need to socialise. She could hardly show off to Sima, she could however use her palace to invite guests. Not only would she then have her audience, but she would also have Sima and the servants at *Ganjbaran* to attend to them. How Sima would feel about having more guests could not have been further from Jima's mind. Jima opened the door of her room and went downstairs. She spent an hour looking in vain for the phone – by chance, she stumbled upon it when she had given up searching. She picked up the handset, and dialled a Villefranche number in France, but instead of her niece's voice, she heard a Kashmiri operator greeting her with an '*Adab arz hai*'. These were the only words Jima understood, as the operator continued speaking in Kashmiri. Jima asked the operator to speak in English, and thus put herself in an impossible situation, as neither she nor the operator spoke any comprehensible English.

However, Jima managed to find a way to have the operator call her niece Mandana in France.

While Jima was on the phone Sima arrived from the garden and saw Jima holding the receiver. She asked her sister who she was talking to, but the latter paid no heed to her question and continued to talk to Mandana. As soon as Sima heard Mandana's name, she furiously gesticulated to Jima to end her conversation. Mandana was Farshid's daughter, and Sima despised her brother. Sima could not believe her ears, or rather prayed that she was mishearing Jima inviting Mandana over. This time she told Jima aloud to hang up. Unperturbed, Jima continued telling Mandana to put the ceremonies aside and accept. Sima's face had turned red from anger. Overwhelmed, she placed her hand on the hook and cut Jima off.

Sima, so annoyed at Jima for having furtively usurped control of *Ganjbaran*, wanted her out. Jima was capable of inviting all the brothers that Sima so passionately disliked. After folding several table cloths, she recovered from her anger and made herself a rose petal and dried lemon infusion. Cup in hand, she then went to the garden to take some deep breaths of the fresh Himalayan air – she found this therapeutic and an effective way to set aside her worries, albeit momentarily.

It was getting dark and it was not wise for anyone to leave the palace alone. The nature surrounding *Ganjbaran* was beautiful, but it was also the habitat of dangerous wild animals. While Sima returned inside to give orders to her domestics, Jima headed towards the woods, leaving from the main entrance in order to avoid Sima. After she had walked about half a league from the palace, something shiny caught her eyes. Her curiosity made her stop and think. What she presumed to be an inanimate object was in fact a snake, which upon feeling a human presence rolled itself up. Jima was about to have a heart attack. While she was stepping away to leave, she accidentally flicked a stone onto the terrifying reptile. Afraid of running into another beast, she sped back to the palace. Once inside, she went upstairs to her room, where she decided that the recent chilling experience had been nothing but an event of her imagination – merely a nightmare that no longer affected her. She fell asleep and thus missed her sister's call to join her for dinner. Sima, supposing that Jima was upset with her and for this reason capriciously refusing to appear, did not bother to look for her and dined alone.

The next morning, Sima thought she would make some morello cherry jam. A servant helped her with the sterilising of the jars and containers. It was still very early in the morning and Jima was still asleep, dreaming of her daughter, Mona. In her dream Mona's face metamorphosed into Mandana's, who offered then Jima her hand. Both women ran into the fields and stumbled over a stone. They were catapulted into a well filled with emerald eyed snakes. Jima's dream was interrupted at that moment by the honk of a vehicle. She woke up.

Jima looked outside the window, and saw Sima heading towards a car. The driver handed Sima a telegram, it announced the arrival of her niece Mandana. Sima took rather badly to this news. She was aghast at the haste with which Mandana had rushed to India. She returned inside and almost piled her tired self to the sofa. She thought she was in one of those inescapable nightmares where everything went wrong. She paused for a while, took a deep breath, and then reasoned with herself. She realised that she barely knew Mandana. She had projected the hatred she had for her older brother to her niece. Mandana might be very different to him. Nonetheless, Sima was still upset – she realised she was more upset with Jima for acting in her usual inconsiderate and autocratic manner.

Jima was still leaning on the window frames, enjoying the views and beauty of the Indian garden. Although she had slept for over fifteen hours, she still felt sleepy and could barely keep awake. With a lot of effort, she dragged herself towards the bathtub and turned on the tap. As she was still sleepy, she thought that her eyes were misleading her when she saw no water running. Finally, realising that she was not to have a shower, she came out of her room and screamed as loud as she could. The servants who were nearby shivered at hearing her scream. Sima fell off her sofa and rushed to the direction of the scream. Rolling her eyes once she realised Jima was not in danger, Sima led her sister to another bathroom.

Half an hour later, Jima came down the stairs with a hat decorated with a collection of yellow fabric hyacinths. Descending the dramatic staircase Jima attempted to sing an operatic verse, but instead of impressing anyone she appeared more ludicrous than ever. In her mind she was performing an opera sung by Maria Callas as professionally as the talented opera singer herself, while she was sounding like an anxious rooster who had spotted a predator. All the servants had gathered around the stairways to gawk at Jima - they had never come across such a spectacle. However, as Indians are generally tolerant and have continuously been exposed to the most eccentric of foreigners throughout the ages, none of them laughed. Sima walked towards the staircase and cried:

"*Jima, please end your performance so that my personnel can return to their daily tasks.*"

At five-o-clock another car appeared. A beautiful young lady with long black curly hair stepped out of it. Her arms, neck, ears, and fingers were all covered with gold. She was dressed as if she was heading for a safari. She went up the steps leading to the main entrance of the palace, pushed the big wooden door, and walked down the corridor until she saw Sima in an adjacent room. Sima, sleeves rolled up and busy decorating her palace, failed to notice the young lady enter. The young lady approached Sima and said with a merry voice:

"*Aunty Sima, your niece is here.*"

Mandana's voice startled Sima, who had no reason to anticipate anyone approach her so unexpectedly. She was hardly able to utter Mandana's name and turned so pallid that Mandana was left wondering what had caused such reaction in her aunt – '*was she annoyed to see her?*'- Mandana thought while apologising to her aunt for having startled her. Soon, the two women were sitting on a comfortable sofa and began catching up with family events and gossips.

After a short while Jima entered looking for Sima, and was gladly surprised to see that next to her sister sat Mandana. She approached her niece and embraced her.

"*I am so happy to see both of you,*" said Mandana. "*Thank you for inviting me to Ganjbaran. You can't imagine how depressed I was. I had just broken up with my boyfriend and I needed to leave the Côte d'Azur as soon as possible. Before reaching the palace, I thought I wouldn't be able to stay long in India, one hears so many horror stories about the poverty in this country, but manifestly it all seems to be based on prejudice. This place is magnificent and I am definitely going to extend my stay.*"

A Young Woman's Dilemma

After a long discussion, Mandana quizzed her aunt about the social life in the vicinity. She clarified that a young single girl like her should be constantly exposed to eligible bachelors. Sima said to her niece:

"There is nothing going on in the area. There are only poor peasants in the nearby village, you should go to New Delhi where there are embassies and exclusive clubs."

"You know aunty Sima, I have been to a number of receptions organised for diplomats in London and Bern and, believe me, embassies are no husband outlets. All the diplomats are so used to having their expenses coverd by their government that they have lost the habit of reaching for their wallets and courting women. I associate embassies with odious agents who work behind counters and who issue visas to the unlucky citizens of the Third World. And the exclusive clubs are filled with retired old men who have forgotten their age and think they can still seduce a young woman like me. I am looking for romance not pensioners and cheapstakes."

Jima intervened:

"My dear Mandana, don't worry. Not far from the palace near Srinagar, there is a Military Club which my father mentioned to us on several occasions. I am very curious to see it. One day we can go there together."

"Our father had lived during the colonial period," Sima reminded them with a smile, *"and the building of the Military Club has been turned into a brothel. However, Mandana, you still have the chance to meet men over there."*

Mandana was offended by Sima's comment, as she thought that Sima was referring to her promiscuous lifestyle. She believed that Sima intended to insult her. Sima herself was far from being chaste and Mandana was fully aware of this. She therefore turned to Sima and said:

19

"My beloved aunt, I am far less experienced than you are. That sort of men wouldn't even consider me, if they knew you were in the vicinity."

Jima, conscious that this exchange could escalate to such extent as to undermine her free holiday at Sima's, and possibly lead Sima into throwing her and their niece out, intervened:

"My adorable niece, I have had a beautiful room prepared for you."

Sima, worrying that the antique furniture may have been damaged during the move, asked anxiously:

"I hope you have not had any furniture moved from one room to another?!"

Jima did not even bother to reply, this time not out of her usual arrogance but to avoid revealing that an old lamp had been accidentally broken whilst she was helping a maid move a cupboard.

Mandana thanked Jima and said:

"You are such a wonderful aunt."

Jima uttered a strange hen-like noise, to demonstrate her satisfaction. She then accompanied her niece to the first floor, and while they were climbing the stairs, Jima said:

"Don't worry about finding a suitable husband. This is an extraordinary palace, bound to attract extraordinary visitors. It has already brought us here. You will see, Ganjbaran is going to be a place of many fond memories for us."

Mandana sighed:

"Extraordinary phenomena, such as ghosts appearing and statues speaking, are more likely to happen here than any handsome man landing beside me."

"If you truly believe in this man, then he would materialise."

"The Jews and Muslims have believed in a god for centuries, but he has never materialised," retorted Manadana with a smile.

"People are free to believe in whatever they want and err for generations, but we shouldn't follow their example. Our gods are tangible and we can witness the form of our divinities through their statues. The power of faith is immense. Unless you don't believe that you will be married one day, don't expect a bridegroom to stand beside you in the years to come."

Jima was alluding to the secret creed of her family. The Gilipours were conscious of the dangers to which they would have exposed themselves had they expressed their religious beliefs to their neighbours in Tehran. During the reign of the Shah, people in the city might have regarded them as eccentrics, but in previous centuries they might have been executed on grounds of polytheism. The Islamic revolution revived old prejudices and created such an intolerant atmosphere for religious groups not recognised by the regime that the Gilipour family had no choice but to leave. Jima was afraid that due to isolation the new generation of her family would loose their ancestral faith. She could see that the youngsters were more interested in mundane life rather than spiritual matters. Indeed, at that particular moment, Mandana was more interested in her bedroom and the view from its window, than in gods.

After Mandana had seen her room she went with Jima to the garden to have a walk before dinner. Sima asked them not to go too far as the meal was practically ready. The two women were pleased to hear this and, returned to the kitchen after a quarter of an hour. While Sima was pouring the pomegranate paste on to the chicken, Jima asked her niece about her father, Farshid. Mandana said:

"I have not seen him for a long time. He commutes between Zurich and London and I live by myself in Villefranche."

"Mandana, what about you?" asked Sima. *"Have you finished your studies or are you still completing your university degree?"*

Sima had the habit of asking people about their educational background. Her obsession with degrees and diplomas was due to her own academic setbacks. She could not even spare her niece the question.

"I have quit studying," answered Mandana. *"I already have had a hard time getting the French Baccalaureat. Now I want to enjoy life."*

Jima began lecturing her niece:

"A young woman of your age should live in a healthier environment than the French Riviera. You should have followed your father to London or Zurich where there are more opportunities for a young woman like yourself, and studied something. A life with no goal is a purposeless life – it has no meaning. If you are already living the life of a retired person, what will you do when you are sixty? It's very irresponsible of Farshid to leave you without the supervision of an elder in south of France. While he is glued to his bonds and stocks, you are wasting your youth. You see, Sima, my calling Mandana should be regarded as a blessing to the family. Now that you are here, my adorable niece, I am going to guide you."

"*I am planning to redecorate all the rooms and embellish the gardens,*" said Sima. "*I would need to hire extra staff to keep the place in order. Mandana could work for me and help me manage my staff.*"

"*But you have already Chetra for that purpose,*" Mandana reminded her aunt. "*I suggest you start a cosmetic firm and make me the vice-president. With all the exotic plants here, I am sure we can produce wonderful creams and perfumes.*"

Sima was not impressed with her niece's suggestion:

"*No one would make you vice-president gratuitously. You have to pull up your sleeves, take off your make up and prove yourself to whoever you believe can recruit you. I only hire competent and hard-working people. I advise you to pack your things and go to Pune right away and register at the university. You have to demonstrate your aptitude to me.*"

Jima interrupted her sister:

"*Stop meddling with people's lives. Since your childhood you have been poking your nose into people's affairs and through your silly advice you have turned their lives to sheer hell. How do you think a young woman of Mandana's level could survive alone in Vuna? I have not even heard of that place. She should go to a university near her relatives' place of residence; otherwise she might go astray.*"

Mandana was not interested in discussions about education and universities. Like Jima, she had never heard of Pune, and did not know which aunt had pronounced its name correctly. Seeing that dinner was still not ready, she asked one of the servants to bring a big basket of exotic fruits to the garden, towards which she was walking. There she sat beside a round table covered with a tablecloth with floral designs. She grabbed a big bunch of grapes and ate some until she noticed the silhouette of a person.

It was dusk and the lights of the garden were not yet lit. Mandana was not able to detect who it was. Her curiosity led her to approach the figure, but it was too dark to see anything. The person disappeared from Mandana's sight only to appear again, but this time much closer. The lights of the garden went suddenly on, and the stranger greeted her. Mandana was somewhat puzzled. As the stranger spoke to her in Persian, she knew that the woman was a family member, but she was still unable to recognise her, so she greeted the newcomer hesitantly.

At this moment, Sima came out onto the porch to see Mona talking to Mandana. She was practically certain that Mandana did not remember her cousin. Mona was relieved to see Sima and ran towards the porch. Sima kissed and hugged her. Mandana could not fail but notice how warmly Mona had been received. She herself had not been welcomed so genuinely.

While Mandana was climbing the stairs towards the two other women, Mona said:

"*I recognised Mandana from the family pictures, but I am not sure if Mandana remembers me.*"

Mona then paused and looked at Mandana, hesitating to hug her, but Mandana took the initiative and welcomed her cousin to *Ganjbaran*.

Sima said:

"*While you two are getting acquainted with each other, I am going to give Jima the good news.*"

A Vain Hope

Later in the evening Sima and Mandana stood in the kitchen while Chetra was preparing the dinner. She was making an Indian dish, and the two Iranian women were attentively watching the cook to check that she did not put chilly in their food. In order to accelerate the cooking process, Sima put on an apron and opened a cupboard beside an arabesque window. She asked Mona if she could see any serving dish. Mandana's eyes fell on a glossy purple oval bowl which reminded her of the bowls sold in the markets of Liguria. She picked the bowl and handed it to her aunt, who poured the cooked lentils into it. There were three big baskets nearby. One of them contained fresh mint, shallots and radishes. Another basket contained coriander, tarragon and basil. The last basket was filled with dried aromatic herbs. On small wooden shelves, fixed on the wall, stood small bottles containing various spices.

Mandana was not used to working in the kitchen, but the excitement of being in an Indian palace surrounded by relatives encouraged her to participate in the domestic chores. She had made many resolutions in the past, such as taking piano or accounting lessons - she did neither. She had heard that India had the power of transforming people, and was counting on this trip to be metamorphosed. Indeed, many people who had travelled around India and experienced India's culture in depth had turned into different beings. Mandana's experience of India, on the other hand, was limited to a sojourn in her aunt's luxurious palace, and yet, she was expecting to change.

In the south of France, she used to spend her days with different boyfriends – men of different ages. She spent hours in cafés and restaurants, and ended her nights in discos, if it was not in the bed of a bachelor or a divorcee.

Mandana had no other goal but to get married, and thought that upon seeing her adopting decent habits, the gods would grant her her wish.

During her trip from Nice to New Delhi, she had a stop in Istanbul. There, she had met a thirty-year old English man. He was tall, blond, blue-eyed with a pinkish skin, and probably considered quite average looking in England, but he was just as Mandana imagined the man of her dreams. She had smiled at him, and they had ended up exchanging telephone numbers. Inadvertently, she had put the piece of paper containing the young man's phone number inside her passport, and while she was passing through the Turkish customs the paper had slipped, and fallen on a Turkish officer's lap. By the time Mandana realised the incident, she was already on the plane drinking martinis. She thought she had missed the chance of her life. She hoped that the potential suitor would contact her in the very near future.

Mandana recounted her story to Sima, who advised her to forget the flirt:

"Nowadays, men have become so stingy that they don't even bother sending their girlfriends flowers for their birthday. And you think that this chap is going to call you long distance from England or come to India with the sole intention of seeing you? If at least he knew that you were a rich heiress, you could have kept some hope, but in these circumstances, you have far greater chances of finding a cave full of precious gems than this man coming after you."

An Unusual Mother

While Sima and Mandana were roaming in the kitchen, Mona started unpacking in her room. She was happy to be at Sima's and had no intention of returning to London soon. The last months in England had been difficult for her. She needed affection and considered Sima's invitation a blessing.

Filled with feelings of tenderness, she went to her mother's room and saw her lying on the bed. Mona had been away from her family for such a long time that she had forgotten that her mother had no maternal instincts. She waited until Jima woke up and asked her whether she could come and help her unpack. Jima was in no mood to do such a thing and suggested that Mona call one of the domestics instead.

"*They are paid to do such things, you know.*" After she said this, Jima glanced at her daughter and noted that the young woman appeared sad. Ordinarily, Jima had little concern about other people's state of mind, but as Mona was her daughter, she tried to appear concerned – but still, couldn't bring herself to get out of bed. She therefore said to Mona:

"*My adorable daughter, you look pale. Don't you want to go downstairs and take some aspirins with some herbal tea? You would feel much better afterwards.*"

Mona sat on her mother's bed and said that she was too tired to go downstairs:

"*I would rather lie down here.*"

Jima moved a little on her bed in order to make space for Mona to rest. While Mona was lying beside her, Jima thought it a good opportunity to satisfy her curiosity. She wondered why Mona had come to India without her children. She interrogated her, but Mona sought to postpone discussing something that was clearly a topic she would rather not talk about, and told her mother that it was a long story that she would share with her another time.

"*My adorable daughter,*" said Jima, "*you sound a bit tormented. You shouldn't worry about a thing. Nothing is worth ruining your health for in this world.*"

Listening quietly to her mother's soothing words, Mona began to feel serene and somewhat loved. Mona's silence, however, was disturbing Jima. She felt as if her daughter was transferring her anxiety to her. "*What is the point of having her beside me, if she refuses to talk?*" thought Jima, and decided instantly to roll over and push forcefully the young woman out of her bed. Mona fell to the floor and landed squarely in reality. She realised she had been naïve to have expected her mother to change. As she could witness, Jima was as selfish and inconsiderate as before. Mona ran downstairs crying like a child, hoping to get consoled by her aunt.

A Call from Abroad

Night was approaching Kashmir. The moon was half way up in the sky but the radiant sun still dominated its vault. The four women had by now finished dinner, when Mandana's father, Farshid, called from Switzerland.

Jima rushed to answer the phone. As Farshid was responsible for Mandana's expenses, he had been informed of his daughter's visit to India thanks to her credit card statements. For more than an hour, Jima talked nonsense, bragging continuously about her invisible possessions, and amid all the bragging she completely forgot that by inviting Farshid to *Ganjbaran*, she would trigger a war in Kashmir.

Farshid, though not as rich as Sima, was quite well off, and therefore it was expedient to Jima to be in good terms with him. Should she fall out with Sima, Jima wanted to keep her options open in term of places to stay. However, unlike Sima, Farshid was not too keen on having guests stay over – he was more partial to being generous to those who flattered him and made him feel important. Jima could not play that game – not out of any moral qualms, but because of her own vanity. Although vanity rarely obfuscated her strategic thinking, in this case it eclipsed her intention of praising Farshid - she ended up talking about her own imaginary achievements, and went into a characteristically protracted monologue. Farshid had enough of Jima's voice and interrupted her, asking to speak to Sima. Jima felt insulted and hung up.

Farshid tried to call back several times but the connection was poor and he could hardly be heard.

By this stage, Sima felt as if she was in a nightmare, but marginally relieved that, should she be in one, there was hope of waking up and out of it.

Jima virtually behaved as the mistress of the house. She shamelessly said that if Farshid had something important to share, he would continue to call until he got connected. Jima then continued to speak about her past glorious days, but Sima and Mandana, fed up by now, were too annoyed to stay in the room and headed towards their bedrooms. Mona was already upstairs. Jima did not see any point in remaining by herself, and left also.

The Pleasures of Gossiping

Before going to bed, the servants turned off all the lights of the ground floor leaving on only the ceiling lamp of the main hall for security reasons. Two men had come from the village as nightguards to watch over the palace, but in fact spent the entire night just talking to each other, being little concerned about the residents' security.

On the first floor, Jima had put on her nightgown and was sitting sleepless on her bed. The other three women, once they had got rid of Jima and had brushed their teeth, gathered in Mona's room - to share their memories, to gossip about the rest of the absent family, and to get to know each other better. They revelled in discussing the shortcomings of their other relatives.

Sima drew up a list of adulterous aunts and female cousins. Mona opened her heart and named the people against whom she held a grudge. It was a typical family gathering during which everybody felt at ease to trust another and reveal family secrets till then undisclosed. The discussion went even further. Personal secrets, which would one day be divulged at the expense of the confessor, were being shared. Mandana was candidly recounting her love affairs and confirming the rumours that she had slept with countless men. The poor girl was unaware that her words were going to be spread around in another continent to the delight of other idle gossipers. Mandana, however, was bravely defending her lifestyle, saying that she did not understand why virginity was such an issue in their society, she declared:

"It isn't fair. Why should a girl remain a virgin until her wedding night? In the same way that the Jews circumcise their boys at birth, we should deflower newborn girls."

Mona, who had left the country much earlier than the other women, had less knowledge of the family affairs. She needed more details. There were a few relatives she had never met in her life. Though she was following the discussion and enjoying the gossip immensely, she was the least involved, and as a consequence she soon fell asleep. The other two women were finding it difficult to leave Mona's room and let the young woman sleep in peace. Whenever one of them reminded the other that they had better return to their room, one would hastily add a concluding sentence, and so the conversation went on. They were all conscious that this sort of discussion seldom arises and even more seldom is reignited as uninhibitedly and casually as it arose that evening, and as such the women were hesitant to draw the gossiping to a close.

When finally they managed to leave Mona to rest, it was very late and indeed the holy sun was conquering the sky again. As Sima and Mandana had not duly accepted the god of Sleep's invitation when it was time to do so, he consequently turned a deaf ear to their plea for sleep. Insomniac, they lied in their beds.

The Story of a Betrayed Wife

At six-o-clock in the morning Sima decided to leave her room. Shattered from the lack of sleep, she went into the garden to cut some flowers for the breakfast table. She was too tired to notice where she was going and what she was cutting. Her property was so vast that there were parts where no one had set foot for years. In the early hours of the day, these corners still appeared spooky. She failed to detect an ancient stone with engraved images of gods and Sanskrit scripture. She just walked over it and returned to the palace with a big bunch of flowers.

Sima asked Chetra to set the breakfast table. Chetra called the two male servants, and asked them to bring the small boxes of citrus fruits from the cellar, while she placed Indian *paneer* cheese, butter and sliced cucumbers on the table. Sima lit the samovar she had brought from Iran for the tea. Her grandmother's samovar had been given to Atoossa, Sima's eldest sister. This one was an old Russian samovar she had found at the bazaar of Ardebil.

Around seven in the morning, a man in rags brought fresh baked *naan* breads from the village along with milk and cream, and handed them to Chetra. The only things that were missing were honey and jam. Sima asked Chetra to bring the quince and morello cherry jams Mandana had purchased in Istanbul. Soon after, Jima entered and complimented her sister for setting a beautiful breakfast table, however, her tone and manners were condescending, as Jima believed that by being condescending, somehow, she was conveying her superiority. Finally, Mona and Mandana joined the other two women and they all started having breakfast. The scent of rosewater that emerged from the quince jam was overwhelming and Jima could not deny herself the pleasure of inhaling it.

Once Jima had finished eating, she asked her daughter why she had not brought her children to India. As soon as Jima finished her phrase, Mona burst into tears.

Sima and Mandana went towards Mona to comfort her, but Jima stayed at her place and said:

"My well-bred daughter, instead of answering such a simple question, you react like a child. You have inherited these stupid attitudes from your father. All his family were abnormal."

Mandana reacted to her aunt's comments:

"How can you be so insensitive?" And she turned to Mona and continued: *"You are sitting in the middle of a beautiful palace, surrounded by your family - people who love you. You should enjoy these moments. You should share your sorrow with us. We can pull you through it. I am sure that things are not as bad as you imagine them. Perhaps if you were having a wonderful time in London, you might not have even considered coming to India. Every cloud has a silver lining."*

Mona, tearful still, said that it was hard for her to recount her story. Mandana gave a sigh and said she wished she had some amusing relatives around to cheer Mona. Sima turned to Mandana and said:

"The next person who invites people to my palace without my permission will be thrown out."

Mandana was not a person to sit back and listen when she felt mistreated. She responded right away:

"You sound like a parvenu Sima. How many times per day do we have to hear you affirm your ownership of this palace? My father owns mansions in different parts of Europe, and has never felt the need to mention this to anyone. It's time you got off your high horse."

Jima interrupted Mandana and began admonishing Sima too, as she held old grudges against her. Mona was forgotten. The poor woman stopped crying. The scene stunned her. After a short while, Mandana turned to Mona as she was curious to know what was going on in her cousin's life, and said:

"While these two sisters are arguing, tell me what is wrong."

Mona took a deep breath and started her story:

"One early morning, a torrential rainfall woke me up. It was still dark, but I decided to get out of bed. I went towards the window and there I saw my husband,

Karl, opening the door of his car. I wondered where he was going. It was five-o-clock in the morning; too early for him to be going to work. I thought that it had been a long time since I had last seen Karl in the morning."

Mandana interrupted Mona:

"Don't you wake up when he is getting ready?"

Mona replied:

"We don't share the same room any longer. That is another story. But to continue, that morning I felt a bit suspicious seeing Karl leave so early, and some mysterious force was pushing me to follow him. Don't get me wrong- I am not the type of woman who keeps a close watch on her husband. Till that day it had never occurred to me to follow Karl. I did not even dress up or have breakfast, I just put on a coat, which I realised later was Karl's. I took the keys of my car and raced out. I started the car frantically and pressed the accelerator as hard as I could to catch up with Karl. Karl drove quite fast and it was hard for me to keep up with him, but just as I decided to give up, Karl turned into a road and stopped in front of a small villa. He did not even notice my car, he went straight towards the villa and just as he was about to knock, a blond woman, practically naked, with only a shawl around her hips, came out of the house and jumped like a vulture on him, touching and kissing him all over. I felt like I had swallowed a bitter pill, and all my throat and lungs were burning. I was not able to think properly, I just started the car and drove back home. I was angry at myself - I felt stupid and worthless. I thought that I deserved this. I started questioning myself: why would Karl ever want to end up with a woman like me. Nature had given him everything. Apollo had shaped him in his own image, whereas I, like Medusa, had only incurred the gods' wrath. But why had he chosen a harlot, as, surely, a woman who roams around naked can't be anything more? I was in desperate need of love and support. As I was opening the door I heard the telephone ringing. I hurried in. I did not want to miss the call, especially since at that moment I really needed to talk to someone. The gods were with me; fate wanted the call to be from the land where they are worshipped the most. You don't know how happy I was to be invited by Sima to India. At that time, I had just one idea in mind and that was to leave England. I wanted to be with family. I knew that I could find this comfort in India, but still I did not know if I should take my children with me, and I really did not want to leave them with Karl. So before starting to pack, I telephoned Azar, our grandmother's niece in Canada. I planned to send them to her, because she is known to be a responsible person and a dedicated mother.

Ganjbaran

It was probably around ten in the evening in Vancouver when I called Azar. I was glad that she herself picked up the phone. I did not give her the chance to conduct a polite conversation. I was very uncomfortable and told bluntly that I needed temporarily to send her my children and that I would explain to her my reasons at a later stage. Poor Azar did not know what to say. I could feel that she was not pleased, who would be nowadays? Life in exile involves enough hardship. But I couldn't think of anybody else and the poor woman accepted. Then I rushed to pack, bringing our bags and suitcases down from the attic, something that Karl used to do before our trips. While I was packing something came suddenly to my mind. Some nights Karl used to fix me a drink and very shortly after I felt lethargic and fell asleep. I was wondering if he had been drugging me regularly in order to prevent me from discovering he was having an affair. I was intrigued, and was wondering why he did not ask for a divorce if he loved another woman? Then I thought to myself that I shouldn't jump to early conclusions, maybe I was wrong after all, maybe I had misinterpreted the scene I had witnessed. But when I thought harder, I asked myself what else could it have been besides adultery, after all Karl had left early in the morning in a very furtive way. Even at that moment when I was doubting his fidelity, I did not feel that I would be leaving him. Ever since I met him, I have been enticed by his physical appearance. Everyday I nourished my eyes by looking at his celestial blue eyes and his heavenly complexion. He was always in my mind and always in my dreams. Whenever he was beside me, I thought I was living a fairytale. He was so self-confident, that wherever we went we always received special attention. Whenever I was running my errands by myself, no one even noticed me. I said to myself that if I really loved him, I should leave him so that he could find somebody he deserved. Thinking that way it became easier to finish packing. Som, my elder son, woke up and saw me packing his things, he asked if they were not going to school. I told him that they were going to have fun on the plane instead. Som was pleased to hear the news and jumped to kiss me. Suddenly, something else came to my mind. Karl and I had a couple of joint accounts, I decided to close them and open new accounts so that Karl wouldn't have access to them. After all, I needed the money. I knew that Karl had other accounts of his own and he could manage. I first called the banks and then called airline companies for last minute tickets. As it was early in the morning I thought that I could get the flights I wanted, especially that I was ready to purchase first class tickets. I still felt lost. My whole world had crumbled before my eyes. I was worried that Karl would call one of the banks and become aware of my little scheme. I was daunted by what awaited me if things went wrong. My heart was beating faster and faster. What could I have done if he suddenly entered the house? I might have had a stroke. I quickly called Air Canada. Thankfully I found three tickets for Vancouver, via Toronto, on the very same day. I did not want to send the children alone to Canada, I wanted to accompany them and hand them safely to Azar and then come to India. However, the airline agent told me that I had to hurry if I did not want to miss the flight.

Sima interrupted Mona:

"How old are your children?"

Mona gave a quick answer and continued her story:

"I did not even call a taxi, I took my own car and rushed to the airport, I did not care about leaving my car at the airport's parking, because I had no intention of returning to London. But you don't know what I went through at the airport: Everybody looked like Karl, either from the front or from behind. I was going crazy. Even Som thought he had seen his father through the window of a toy shop, where I refused to linger. I had a guilty conscience and Som was bombarding me with questions. I was not able to take a deep breath until I had boarded that plane. Feelings of hatred, guilt, anger, sadness and insecurity arose in me all at once. I wanted to take my revenge from Karl and at the same time I wanted to return to him. Taking money from our joint account was a vindictive act on my part, but it had not satisfied me. I did not want to leave Karl with that loose woman. I was working hard to forget everything that had happened to me that day. I thought to myself that I should do the utmost to enjoy my trip, especially as I was travelling for the first time in first class, paid by what I considered to be Karl's money."

Jima interrupted Mona to show off:

"I also came to India in first class."

"But the trip did not turn out as well as I wanted," continued Mona, *"Som was sick on my dress, I took him to the lavatory with one of the flight attendants and when I returned to my seat Kouros had thrown up as well. The scene had disgusted one of the passengers sitting across from us and she too had ended up being sick. Just before we landed in Toronto I decided to look at the positive side of my trip, at least all this air sickness had allowed me to forget Karl for a while.*

From the airport in Toronto I called Azar and informed her of our arrival time in Vancouver. She was waiting for us when we arrived. She hugged all of us and before we even set our foot outside the airport, Azar started questioning me, she was dying to know what had made me leave England. Azar's accent is so amusingly spiced with Kermani intonations that I forgave her her curiosity."

Mandana interrupted the long narration:

"Did you know that until two years ago Azar was in San Remo, living an hour's drive away from me?"

"I wonder why so many Iranians left Europe for North America?" Sima then inquired.

"It's probably because North Americans encourage immigration," replied Mandana. *"On my flight to New Delhi an American woman of Greek descent recited to me the beautiful verses written on the walls of the Statue of Liberty: 'Give me your tired, your poor, ...; send these the homeless, tempest-tost to me, I lift the lamp beside the golden door.' She told me that this is the spirit upon which America has been built. The verses should say it all."*

Jima said that all those beautiful verses were made of empty words:

"The Americans don't honour a single line of that sonnet. I went for an interview at the American Embassy in Turkey, and the ambassador refused me a tourist visa, because I have an Iranian passport. Had I known those verses, I would have recited them to him before leaving his office."

Sima praised Mandana for her memory and said:

"Although I enjoy those verses, I agree with Jima. It's hypocritical of the American government to put them there, since so many immigrants are turned back, and so many people have suffered in the United States. How can they call it a golden door, when blacks suffered slavery there and many natives were exterminated?"

Mona was less interested in politics than in her mother's plan to go to the States. She asked Jima why she had not been informed about her decision. Sima led all of them back to the original subject and asked Mona:

"How long are you going to leave the children with Azar and when are you planning to inform Karl?"

Mona said she was not worried about her children, as Azar had brought up two boys and knew how to handle them. She added:

"I invited Azar to India, and asked her whether she would perhaps consider living here. She said that she would love to visit Sima's palace, but that she would rather live in Canada as it offers more opportunities to youngsters than anywhere else and told me that a Canadian passport is more sensible to get than an Indian one. She then added that Indians themselves migrate to Canada, why then would she move to a country whose own people leave."

Sima was not pleased with Mona's ultimate revelation - she was angry that Mona had invited Azar to India without consulting her. She was so irritated that she addressed Mona in an austere and bitter tone:

"You are a selfish and inconsiderate woman. I don't care whether you are happy to have your children with Azar or not. I am interested to know how Azar feels about being treated like a cheap nanny, and how Karl feels about having his children kidnapped by his wife. And now you are sitting in front of us, and playing the innocent."

Mona did not expect such a reaction, she thought that she was the only victim and deserved everyone's sympathy. She did not know what to say, so she burst into tears. Sima did not feel like consoling Mona any more, her whole opinion about her niece had changed after what she had heard. Even Mandana was confused, since Mona had the reputation of being candid and shy, though on reflection, Mandana realised that it may have all been a façade since Mona was no softy. After hearing Sima, Mandana came to the conclusion that she deserved more pity than Mona, since with all her beauty she had remained single, while her ugly and depressing cousin had married a rich and handsome man.

Mona continued crying, telling the others that they did not know how it felt to be separated from one's own children and be cheated on. Jima suggested to Sima to call Azar and have Mona talk to her children. Sima did not know what to do. She really did not feel like doing Mona any favour, but if she did not call, who knows what nasty stories would have been said behind her back. Her calling Azar for Mona was not even going to be considered by the others as a favour but a duty. She picked up the telephone reluctantly and called Azar.

It took a while before she was connected. The operator through which she was calling was acting bizarrely and Sima was wondering if he understood English at all. Sima held the receiver for Mona without even talking to Azar, but Mona did not take the receiver from her; she was too busy crying. Jima took over and began talking chiefly about herself so much so that she forgot why she had originally called and kept on in the usual fashion to talk about what she considers to be the most fascinating subject – her nonexistent wealth and unachieved achievements.

While Jima was glued to the phone, Sima left the room. The four new servants had come to see her in order to tell her that they would not be able to work in the coming weeks as they had to take care of their crops now that autumn was approaching. Sima insisted on keeping Chetra by offering to triple her wage - Chetra accepted.

Understanding Men

The Sun was shining high in the sky. The end of summer was approaching. It had been a particularly dry summer. The inhabitants of Kashmir were desperate for rain, since their lands had gone arid and not a single grain was growing. The peasants, like the domestics working for Sima, were particularly hit by the drought. They were so broke that they were considering selling their land – their only source of sustenance in a state without welfare – in order to survive on whatever they received in exchange from the opportunistic buyers. While these poor peasants had problems irrigating their lands, a spring spurted right in front of Sima's courtyard, her land was so fertile that many trees of *Ganjbaran* were so laden with fruit, that their branches touched the ground. Such was the mysterious aura safeguarding the fabulous estate.

Sima returned from Srinagar, where she had gone to discuss her finances at the City council. She found Mona and Mandana sitting together on the porch. Mandana was consoling and advising Mona. Men were Mandana's favourite topic. Although she considered Mona more skilled than herself in dealing with men, she still felt the urge to share her experiences with somebody. In a way she could relate more to Mona than anybody else in the palace, since she came closest to her age and at the time she was the only one experiencing problems with a man.

Mandana told Mona that she understood perfectly how she felt:

"*I myself have been in a similar situation before. I once had a boyfriend who wasn't only gorgeous, but was also rich, intelligent and well-mannered. I was practically sure that he was going to be my future husband, but then I found out that there were other women in his life. Although I was aware of my boyfriend's unfaithfulness I wasn't able to leave him because I was convinced that I would never find anyone like him. Finally, one day my handsome boyfriend announced his engagement to another woman and said they were going to get married in a month. At that moment I felt that for him I was nothing more than a bird's dropping. After his wedding to which, as you can imagine, I wasn't invited, he called me again to sleep with me; he told me that he had to limit his visits to half an hour, just enough time for opening his 'bottle of champagne', as he put it. I was then dating Giovanni, an Italian guy from Milan, therefore I really felt no need to sleep with him. So I just told my ex, stop saving money and call an escort instead. Later I found out that he was cheating on his wife with two other women, one of whom he left pregnant. I was relieved that I wasn't the one he had chosen to marry."*

Mona listened attentively to Mandana's story without interrupting her, but was not impressed by it, as she could not relate to it at all. She said:

"Mandana, you can't compare Karl with your horny boyfriend."

Sima, who had been eavesdropping, barged in:

"Indeed, Mandana. Listening to your story, I gather the guy did not love you. He just wanted a couple of good nights. But Karl loves Mona since he married her. Moreover, they have had two children together. Mona has to fight to keep him. How many wealthy, educated, handsome, professionally successful men can you find out there? Our world is full of wild women waiting for an opportunity to snatch such rare species. They don't care whether they are married or not. You see, men are like children; they fall for whoever shows them two big balloons." Then turning to Mona, Sima continued, *"Don't worry, my dear, you were wise to leave him momentarily and to come to India. He had taken you for granted. Now that he is left alone, he will have the chance to ponder his relationship with this woman, and he will soon realise that big balloons are not sufficient to build a future."*

"But Sima," said Mona, *"my coming to India wasn't planned for a particular effect - I certainly wouldn't want to be with a man who doesn't want to be with me."*

"Listen, young lady," replied Sima, *"women have a lot of power over men. Men have gone to war for women, cities have been destroyed for women. The endless Trojan war was triggered because of a woman. If you don't use this power, you will fall behind others who will."*

Mandana, who was immensely enjoying the conversation, felt that she should show her relatives that they are treading into her "field of expertise" and that they should follow her advice. She turned to Mona and said:

"Our aunt is a wise woman, and I am not saying you shouldn't listen to her, but she is missing a point here. We well-bred women, coming from decent families, don't know how to play with men. Moreover, we have been brought up in a traditional environment, and have not had the chance to date men overtly. Our mothers did not even have the right to have contacts with men and consequently they have not earned the experience to give us tips on any matter concerning relations with the opposite sex. North American and Northern European women, on the other hand, are able to dominate men, as they have been used to dating boys since their childhood and have also benefited from their mothers' advice who shared their experiences with them. Have you noticed how well average American or English women handle Asian men: they don't cook as often as we do for them, and when they cook they usually make simple dishes, they do whatever pleases them, they even have extramarital affairs if they choose so, and above all when Iranian men marry foreign women they don't care if they are educated or from decent families, they pick the first woman they meet at a strip club or a bar and with all this they always compliment their foreign wife as they are afraid that if they don't show any appreciation, their wife is going to leave them. But when it comes to Iranian or Indian women, Asian men become very fussy. First of all they want their future wife to be a virgin with a huge dowry, then they want her to stay at home raising children and cooking fine dishes every day. With all these expectations, they say that Iranian and Indian women are not good enough."

"We are not dealing with an Asian man here," Sima reminded them. *"We are talking about Karl."*

"What I said previously is still valid: Mona has no experience with men and therefore she doesn't know how to deal with Karl," replied Mandana.

Sima lost her temper and asked Mandana:

"What is your point? Mona has had two children with Karl. She couldn't simply walk away from him."

"I know it's tough, but if she is miserable in this marriage, she will ruin her health. Can you guarantee then that her kids are going to be grateful to her in the future for staying with their father for their sake?" asked Mandana.

"Your advice isn't constructive. Mona might not be an expert in handling men, but she can always learn. With our support and affection, she will be able to take control of her life. She should give her marriage a second chance lest she regrets it later. Only if she concludes that her relationship with Karl is doomed, will she be

able to move on. And to return to your earlier argument, I would add that Asian men give Asian women a hard time, because our societies have allowed them to do so. It's now up to us to set things right and claim the rights that were denied to our mothers. We can only achive this if we were confident and strong. Mandana, you seem to have faired well in this domain. You don't appear to be the type of woman who has been sitting at home waiting for a suitor. Perhaps you can launch a Pan-Asian movement for women's liberation," concluded Sima.

"My dear aunt, I am not convinced that I have faired well. Yes, I have had many boyfriends, if that is what you mean, but it has not got me anywhere. As I said, our culture doesn't prepare women to live in free societies where women can date and get to know men. I am underscoring our issues."

"Well then, I don't know how helpful your suggestions can be, if you are just presenting our shortcomings and don't have any solutions," said Sima gravely.

Mona felt sick and insisted that she wanted to talk about a completely different subject:

"At this moment I am disoriented and need more time to muster up the courage and energy necessary to face my real situation."

Sima offered to go and find Jima and prepare the supper. The three women went downstairs, where they found Jima involved in a deep conversation with what appeared to be flowers. Sima decided to release the flowers from her sister's monologue, and led her to the kitchen.

While they were preparing their dinner, the telephone rang and Sima went to answer. The three other women continued cooking, and when Sima returned from her long phone conversation, dinner was ready on the table and the three other women were waiting for her. Jima asked Sima:

"Who was it that kept you for so long on the phone?"

"I don't want to discuss it now. I will tell you all after the meal," said Sima.

"Was it Azar?" inquired Mona.

Sima was not able to withhold the information any longer. As Sima had expected, Mona had become so anxious in anticipation of the news that her appetite had gone, and she wanted to know every detail of the conversation. Sima therefore had to break the news earlier than planned:

"Karl has found out that Mona has left the children with Azar in Canada (and, turning to Mona) and he now knows that you are in India. According to

Karl, you had inadvertently left Azar's telephone number beside the telephone. According to Azar, Karl had checked with the airlines to find out about your destination, and then called Azar. She said that he was so certain that the kids were with her that she couldn't have possibly lied. I told Azar that she had done the right thing. Now Karl is on his way to Canada. I asked Azar to keep Karl in Canada and to not hand him the children until Mona and I got there."

Mona was so worried she barely touched her meal.

Obliging Gods

Once the three other women had finished eating, Sima said that she was going to book the flights. Jima asked her to buy three tickets. Aware that, were she to refuse to do so, Jima would keep insisting, Sima remained silent and went straight towards the phone. Mandana realised that Sima did not wish to take Jima along and said:

"*Aunt Jima, if you went also away, then I would be left alone in this huge palace. I don't feel like travelling around the world in order to comfort an unfaithful man.*"

Mona, who was also reluctant to travel with Jima, said:

"*Nothing would make me happier than having my mother beside me during all these hard times,*" then quickly supplemented this by saying, "*however, I don't want to be selfish and have Mandana stay all alone.*"

She reminded Jima that she had invited Mandana to India and therefore was under a duty to stay with her. Knowing how selfish her mother was, Mona added:

"*In addition, Canada has nothing interesting – only very cold weather.*"

Jima, who had not really thought about the cold, gave the matter a second thought and decided to remain in India. When Sima came back into the dining room, Jima asked her to cancel her reservation as she had now decided to remain. Sima simply replied "fine" – and obviously there was nothing to cancel.

In the evening Jima came to the conclusion that it was too dangerous for two women to stay alone in the palace. She suggested that she and Mandana should go to Europe whilst Sima and Mona were away. Sima was not too keen on this, as, being too familiar with the workings of her own sister's mind, she could foresee that Jima expected her to fork the bill for her sojourn in Europe. She also knew that she would have to spend a day in New Delhi sorting out her own visa to Canada, and did not want to go through all that hassle to sort out her sister's visa too. Fortunately for Sima the phone rang and spared her another crisis.

It was Farshid, Mandana's father, who called to announce his sudden visit. This was the first time ever that the visit of someone Sima disliked delighted her. This settled Sima's dilemma as Jima now had no excuse to leave India. Sima broke the news to the family. Mandana was really not looking forward to seeing her father.

While each member of the Gilipour family was dwelling on their own mundane problem, the inhabitants of the nearby village were struggling to find clean water. One of Sima's domestics had come to ask Sima whether the villagers could take water from *Ganjbaran*'s stream for their children. Sima had no heart to refuse the Kashmiri man's request; however, before she let him leave she asked the poor man to help Chetra clean the domed reception room. After finishing his task, he asked Sima for his wage and dashed to the village.

Three hours later, the villagers swarmed *Ganjbaran*. This sight sent Mandana, who was sitting on the porch eating grapes, into a screaming frenzy – she was so shocked, she must have screamed for 30 seconds or so. Jima, who was taking a nap woke up, Sima slipped in the tub, and Mona who was wandering around doing nothing, became alarmed, nearly tripped and snapped the heel of her shoe. They all ran to find out what had happened to Mandana. They just found Mandana with a bowl of grapes looking at the miserable appearance of the poor peasants. At their sight, Mona found another excuse to get depressed. Sima could not stand such useless ways of expressing compassion, and scolded Mona:

"If you really feel sorry for these people, don't just sit there looking like a beaten cat. Help them! Come with me to the kitchen, get some baskets and distribute them among the peasants, so that they will be able to collect fruit and vegetables from the trees and the bushes of Ganjbaran."

Mona looked at Sima with a horrified look and broke into tears and then ran off into the palace. Sima called Chetra and asked her to distribute the baskets. She then announced to the villagers that during her absence they were allowed to come and fetch water. On hearing this, Jima fainted on the floor. Sima told Mandana:

"No wonder Mona had such a disgraceful reaction when I asked her to help the people from the village. She inherited her contempt for the poor from her mother."

Mandana slapped Jima hard in the face so that she would recover consciousness again. Jima who had put on an act, felt the slap badly and screamed as loud as she could and insulted Mandana.

"Instead of acting, you had better pray to the god of wind and rain, so that drought will end and the villagers can return to their lands," Mandana said sarcastically.

The commotion went on until late at night. About two in the morning, the villagers made their way back towards their homes. Jima watched the gates of the estate from the window of her room, glad to see them leave. She then spent the entire night reading eulogies from her sacred book to the god of the skies. Her voice kept Mandana awake.

At dawn, Mandana's eyes finally shut from exhaustion. Jima, on the other hand, had been energised by her prayers. She took a quick shower, dressed as quickly as she could and ran into the garden. She walked towards the field where Sima had cut flowers a couple of days earlier. Jima, like her sister, failed to notice the ancient stone with the engraved images of gods and the Sanskrit scripture. Nonetheless, she sensed an aura, some sort of mysterious presence, at that spot. Some divine powers must have guided her towards the stone on which she unconsciously stepped, and looked towards the skies praying once again. Jima's invocation was answered promptly. Lightning struck the earth and torrential rain poured on all of Kashmir.

Jima was ecstatic to see the rain. She ran back towards the palace like a young teenager, rejuvenated by this occurrence. The rest of the family woke up by the lightning. While Sima and Mona left their bedroom, Jima arrived in her room soaked. She changed her clothes and slid into her bed and slept for the rest of the day with a crescent smile on her lips.

Sima and Mona packed while Jima slept. Mandana wrote a long list of cosmetic products, which she commissioned Sima to buy for her while in Canada. Sima was aghast by the length of the list and asked her niece whether she had not come from Europe herself very recently. Mandana replied:

"These are just basic products that I use everyday. I thought that you might have some of them in reserve here and I was surprised to see you had no lavender tonic for removing make-up and no face cream containing pearl extracts for the night."

In the evening, the unruly storm turned into scattered showers and the three women dined without Jima as they had checked her bedroom and seen her fast asleep. Sima and Mona who had planned to leave in the afternoon, were stranded in *Ganjbaran* due to the storm. The three women went to bed early. Sima and Mona were hoping to leave *Ganjbaran* as soon as the rain was over. Mandana did not have many options; she could not even go outside for a walk. There was not much light inside the palace either, therefore, she did not feel like exploring the different wings in the dark. She went to her bedroom, took an exfoliant from her cosmetic case and rubbed it on her face for half an hour before feeling tired and falling asleep.

Jima woke up about four in the morning. She had slept for more than twenty hours. Contrary to the day before, she did her morning ablutions in her usual slow pace and left her room two hours later. She was so hungry that she could not wait for her family to wake up. By the time she set the table for herself, Sima and Mona had arrived in the kitchen. They were so glad to see the table set and to see that the sky had cleared, that they both kissed Jima on both cheeks. They then both hurriedly ate their breakfast as Sima had booked a car to come and take them to the airport. Mandana got up in time to see her aunt and cousin off, and to bid them farewell.

A Difficult Separation

S itting in the taxi which had hardly gone beyond the gates of *Ganjbaran*, Mona looked back with some nostalgia at the resplendent palace which had recently been her home. She reflected on how much she had enjoyed her time there, and on how until that moment she had had no cause to reflect on her blessings – this made her look forward to her return to *Ganjbaran*. During her stay, she had not once truly felt the need to see Karl – she admitted to herself that this was also true in relation to her children. To her, *Ganjbaran* was a dimension beyond ordinary worries and mundane experiences. For her, time had stopped at *Ganjbaran*. Though it was also a place where she had cried her most, paradoxically these were not tears of deeply felt pain. She was in search of affection, and affection she received. Sima had always been there for her, and, quite literally, thanks to her being by her side in the taxi, Mona felt as if that soothing mystery that *Ganjbaran* had been to her was now this blessing that was accompanying them on their trip. By now, the palace was no longer in sight, but in Mona's mind it was everywhere – she had imbibed its atmosphere so viscerally. The plush and fertile landscape of Kashmir appeared more than ever like paradise to her.

Mona began asking herself why she was going to Canada. She had rediscovered her family and its warmth, she did not feel like going back to her lonely life with Karl. Even if her husband was a handsome and pleasant man, there was no longer any connection between them; except through their children. She thought that if her family could give the love she needed, companionship with Karl was both illusory and frightfully unreliable as there was no trust left. For the first time it occurred to her to think of her blessings, and one of them was to have been born in a family and culture where the sun shines in the gardens and in the hearts. People in Northern countries, she felt, lead such individualistic lives – they leave the parental home early, and when they get older, they end up in nursing homes. Most of her neighbours in London hardly invested in their relatives and friends, and focused only on their part-ners. Overwhelmed at this prospect, unconsciously she loudly exclaimed "*I don't want to end up alone.*" – this startled Sima who then said:

"*What happened my dear? You wouldn't end up alone. In a couple of days you and Karl will be reunited and will soon be back to your home in London; and in a few years you will have forgotten all about this misadventure.*"

Mona sighed.

A Detested Father, an Undesired Brother

Jima and Mandana were left alone in the palace with Chetra. The Kashmiri woman was in the kitchen preparing lunch, while the two other women were idly sitting in conversation with one another in the drawing room. They were talking about Farshid.

"*You know Mandana,*" said Jima, "*your father is one of the unhappiest members of our family. I couldn't believe that he did not invite me to go and stay with him when the revolution broke out in Iran.*"

Instead of defending her father Mandana replied:

"*You are lucky that my father did not welcome you, as he is very difficult to bear. He is always ill-tempered, in addition he would have always reminded you that you are living under his roof and therefore have to follow his rules. He is just slightly better than the new rulers of our country. If his own daughter can't live with him, how could you? Sima's hospitality is exceptional. She might have flaws, but who doesn't? She is a very caring and sensitive person. Everyone knows this. That is why we don't feel at exile here.*"

"*You seem to be too fond of Sima.*" grumbled Jima. "*Sima has not hesitated to remind me every day that this is her palace, and wasn't very delighted when I invited you. We don't feel as if we're in exile here, because we are in India. It isn't thanks to Sima.*"

Mandana left Jima to go and check on Chetra in the kitchen. Chetra had made them a Kashmiri dish with lamb and rice, and also made some traditional *naan*. Mandana checked with Chetra whether she had made any salad. Chetra answered her stiffly that she did not have time to make any, and told her to have yoghurt instead. Mandana took offence at Chetra's tone and an argument soon ensued in the kitchen. Chetra did not want to receive

51

orders from Mandana. Jima came in the kitchen believing that she could handle the situation. Chetra was at this time threatening to leave when the telephone rang. Jima asked Chetra in a kind and maternal tone whether she could answer the phone. Chetra reluctantly did so and returned to the kitchen to announce that it was a phone call from New Delhi. Jima went and picked up the receiver. An airport employee informed her that Farshid and two other men were on their way to *Ganjbaran*. Jima wondered who the two other men could possibly be.

Mandana told Jima that his father had all sorts of emotional baggage which made him act in calculated ways for impressing people:

"*He believes that by travelling with his butler and driver, he demonstrates his importance to anyone that cares to notice.*"

"*If this is the case, then your father is most certainly mentally unbalanced.*"

Jima then paused, perhaps conscious of her own hypocrisy. Indeed, had she Farshid's means, she too would have travelled accompanied, flanked by a chambermaid and a nurse.

Early in the afternoon a vintage car drove into Sima's estate and past the magnolia trees which ran along the pathway to *Ganjbaran*. Farshid asked the chauffeur to pull up in order to cut a magnolia blossom before reaching the palace.

Jima and Mandana had decided to stay inside and not greet Farshid at the porch. They were hoping to offend Farshid, and indeed succeeded. The greeting was very cold, but then Jima decided to break the ice and asked her brother how he was doing, and what brought him to India.

"*I sincerely don't know,*" replied Farshid, "*I thought I would come and visit my sisters and daughter here, but it seems that the cold Himalayan winds cause more than just chilly weather.*"

My beloved brother," said Jima, "*you have always had high expectations. Our mother has spoiled you too much because you were her first son. I never understood why we Eastern women are so fond of our male offspring. If I had one, I would have slapped him in the face once a week to toughen him up.*"

Mandana took the opportunity to add:

"*Apparently, you have been slapping Mona instead, although she wasn't a boy.*"

"That is why she isn't spoilt, and is able to cope well in life," justified Jima.

Farshid interrupted:

"Could somebody bring me and my men some refreshments and show to us our rooms."

"My dear brother, we thought that you were coming alone, and therefore we have had only one room prepared for you."

"Tell your housekeepers to prepare two other rooms as my men are very tired," ordered Farshid with notable arrogance.

Mandana replied in an equally unpleasant tone:

"All the servants are away. We have only one housekeeper left who is now preparing our food. If your men want to have a bed to sleep in, they have to roll up their sleeves and clean off the rooms of their choice on the West wing of the palace."

The tension remained throughout the night. Mandana did not bother to hide her true feelings towards her father. She never forgave him for taking her away from her mother when she was only five years old. Mandana's mother was not from a very wealthy family so she could not obtain the custody of her daughter after her divorce from Farshid. Farshid took Mandana only to punish his wife for leaving him – a circumstance which was reflected in his never really showing much affection to his daughter and hardly ever spending any time with her. Mandana was given to the care of a young nanny who was only interested in boyfriends. Perhaps it was her setting such a poor example that led Mandana to later pursue a similar lifestyle as an adult.

When Mandana reached the age of twelve, she was sent to a boarding school. Later on Farshid tried to make it up to Mandana, but in his own way. He just sent her large sums of money. Mandana saw this as her father's duty, and squandered everything he sent to her. She quit studying as soon as she graduated from secondary school and left Switzerland for Villefranche. At the beginning she quite enjoyed her idle life but after a while she felt it was futile. She needed a maternal presence, but Farshid had warned her that if she tried to find her mother he would cease to support her financially.

By coming to Sima, Mandana wanted to prove to her father that she did not need his money any longer. Farshid was conscious of this little act of defiance, and understood well the effect this had on his diminishing control over the lives of others. He was aging and, perhaps as he himself confronted the evident mortality of human existence, he began to feel increasingly more in need of familial affection. It was only now that he wanted to get closer to his daughter, but did not know how. He still believed that it was not too late to salvage whatever was possible of his relationship with Mandana, but found it hard to comprehend her palpable resentment towards him.

It took a long time before dinner was ready. Farshid was irritated, as both he and his men were famished. Farshid asked his men to eat in the kitchen, while he dined with his family in the dining room. Jima was the only one speaking during the dinner, but Farshid was not listening to her. It was as if Jima's voice were just background noise. While Jima was talking, Farshid turned to Mandana and said:

"*I have come here to take you back to Europe.*"

"*You must be out of your mind,*" retord Mandana.

Farshid reacted by slapping Mandana across the face. Jima stopped talking, shocked by the incident. Mandana left the room saying that she never wanted to see Farshid ever again.

Some time later Mandana re-entered the dining room where the butler and the driver were playing backgammon. She asked them where her father was. They told her that he had gone for a walk in the garden. Mandana was on her way to go to the garden when she saw her father enter the domed hall. Mandana snapped at him:

"*When are you planning to leave?*"

"*I have enough of your impertinence. As my daughter you ought to show me respect.*"

"*I don't owe you anything, and in addition I no longer need your financial support – if you are not leaving then I suppose I shall do so.*"

Mandana then went upstairs to pack. Jima entered her room and asked her where she was intending to go in the middle of the night. Mandana said she was going to the village. Jima concerned that Farshid might leave too, and that she would be left alone in the palace said in an equally concerned voice:

"*But Mandana, you don't have any means of transportation. The roads are not safe for a young woman to leave in the middle of the night. You should at least spend the night at Ganjbaran and leave tomorrow morning. The gods are numerous, and all of them powerful. Who knows, maybe they will force Farshid out of the palace and you won't need to leave after all. At this hour, everybody is going to sleep and tonight you are not going to see Farshid any more."*

Mandana found the advice sensible and stayed in her room. The singing of the Kashmiri nocturnal birds, a lullaby to her, led her to fall asleep.

Ganjbaran, the Palace of Prodigies

The following morning, Mandana woke-up at a quarter to five, hurried to get ready and rushed to the kitchen before there would be any chance of Farshid seeing her. Jima had got there ahead of her and had even laid the breakfast table. Instead of bread they had to eat *rasmalai* and *barfi*, as Chetra had refused to bake *naan*. It was too early to have anybody come from the village and bring them any fresh food. After they had finished eating, Mandana said she was ready to leave as she had finished packing the previous night.

"*Before leaving, come with me to the garden,*" pleaded Jima, "*let's go into the world of nature and summon the gods to grant us a boon.*"

She explained that the last time she had prayed there, her prayers had been granted immediately.

"*Do you remember the day the peasants were pouring into the palace? I ran to the garden and found a holy spot. There I raised my hands to the sky and begged the gods for rain.*"

"*Jima, I really don't have time for silly stories,*" scoffed Mandana, "*I want to leave before your brother wakes up.*"

Jima continued as if Mandana had not uttered a word:

"*If I remember well, that spot isn't very far from the forest, and it's filled with yellow flowers. Can you recall how badly it was pouring that day, that even Sima and Mona couldn't leave?*"

As Jima finished her sentence, Mandana got up to leave the kitchen. Jima took her by the arm and insisted that Mandana follow her. Mandana looked into Jima's eyes and saw that Jima genuinely believed in her extraordinary story. She accepted to follow her on the condition that they dash off straight to the garden and quickly returned to the palace, so that if there were no divine signs she would still have some chance of leaving without seeing Farshid.

Mandana and Jima got to the field where Jima had come before for her prayers. Jima started invoking the god of skies. Mandana watched her aunt with a big smile, trying hard not to laugh. But as soon as Jima asked her to pray as well, she felt the presence of a mysterious force.

"*Jima, this place is a bit eerie,*" said Mandana. "*I am not questioning the existence of gods, but I am not convinced that they actually deal with unimportant human beings like us, and our petty requests. Only famous and powerful people are their business. I think that this place is more likely to be haunted by ghosts. If the gods were really interested in us, why wouldn't they demonstrate it to me, here and right now! They can perhaps open a hole in front of us and lead us to a chamber filled with precious stones, so that we can be part of the jetset.*"

Jima was alarmed by Mandana's attitude towards the divine. She took a step back, but then slipped and fell a few meters behind, on her buttocks. It was a painful fall, and she could not get up. Mandana went towards Jima in order to help her. She was about to ask her aunt whether she could manage to walk back to the palace when an old stone board carved with letters in an ancient Indian language caught her attention. Mandana completely forgot about Jima's fall and pointed at the board to her aunt. While Mandana was wondering how much the stone was worth, Jima wished to know whether the stone had some mysterious power. Mandana helped Jima get up, and both women went towards the stone and tried to pick it up. The stone was firmly stuck to the ground; the only thing the two women managed was to rotate it. As soon as the stone rotated 360 degrees, a part of the ground behind them appeared to separate and subside, and a tortuous pit with decaying spiralled stairways leading to an underground passage appeared before their eyes. Both Jima and Mandana were astonished. Jima turned to Mandana:

"*The gods have manifested themselves; I hope that they are not angry at your cynical view of them.*"

"*If they have truly manifested themselves, then they must be leading us to some treasure. So please take the lead and I will follow you downstairs,*" jeered Mandana.

Jima was hesitant, but she remembered what it was that Mandana had challenged the gods to do: '*Open a hole, and lead us to a chamber filled with precious stones,*' – the words seemed to echo in Jima's mind. Despite the darkness of the pit and the poor condition of the stairs, Jima managed to descend encouraged by the idea of finding precious stones. Mandana followed her. Both women went down more than three hundred steps, thinking they would never reach the bottom. Once at the bottom, they saw a dark subterranean passage. Jima touched the materials before her - they felt like bird feathers. The only light came from the top of the pit, and it lit only the stairways. The entire underground corridor was dark. Jima said that perhaps they had better return back to the garden, as they could not do much in the dark. Mandana refused. She said that she had matches with her and she was going to light them one by one until they found something interesting. As she lit one match, she saw a miniature statue standing in a niche. She touched it and realised that it could be moved. She rotated it and the door at the top of the pit shut over their head, but suddenly a line of oil lamps along the passage lit up.

Now both women were truly spooked, as they did not know whether they would ever be able to leave the pit. Mandana wished to see if by rotating the statue once again the door above them would open up; and indeed it did, but all the lamps went off. Relieved that they were not trapped in the pit, Mandana rotated the statue once again, in order to illuminate their surroundings. The two women were now very excited. The underground corridor was fascinating them – it reminded them of Alice in Wonderland.

"*How could these lamps get lit by just turning this statue?*" asked Mandana. "*This place is extremely old, I am sure they did not have the technology to wire the place at the time of its construction.*"

"*Ancient people had knowledge that even today would fascinate the modern scientist,*" replied Jima. "*The pharaohs of Alexandria had a special lantern with a sophisticated lightning system. Esther's mausoleum in Iran had an antique lamp which never went out. Their source of light is still a mystery.*"

Jima and Mandana walked for about ten minutes in the corridor until they saw a statue of an emerald-eyed smiling god. Jima knelt immediately in front of the god to make a wish. Mandana leaned on the wall behind her in order to appreciate the statue of the deity. As her back touched the wall, she

58

realised that it was unstable. She told Jima to get up and push the wall. As soon as the wall rotated the lights on the other side were automatically lit. The two women screamed out of sheer stupefaction. Piles of jewels and precious stones were lying before them. They could not see the floor of the chamber for all the treasure. The gold artefacts were covered with precious stones glowing from every direction: diamonds, rubies, emeralds, sapphires, lay before their eyes.

Jima felt that this finding was clear evidence in favour of the existence, power, and providence of the gods. She was convinced that Mandana too would see it this way, and so she almost challenged her to renounce the incredulity and skepticism she had hitherto demonstrated whenever they happened to discuss anything connected to the divinities.

Mandana was too absorbed by the immense quantity of gems to spare any thought about the gods. She froze at the sight of such astonishing lavishness, and gaped like a fish. Jima, on the other hand, roamed among the gems picking them up spryly. It was as if their discovery, although clearly remarkable and extraordinary, was something possible and therefore not surprising. Jima had never doubted what to her appeared to be the capacity of the gods to perform this sort of miracle. Mandana picked a large diamond from the pile and said:

"Jima, do you think this place really is abandoned? What if these jewels belonged to somebody like in the Ali Baba story."

"Even in the Ali Baba story," answered Jima, *"the owners of the jewels were not known, since they were all stolen. That said, I can't believe that you are asking such a silly question. You questioned the benevolence of the gods earlier, and they delivered to you what you requested. Now you are acting as if even this isn't sufficient proof. You are bound to offend them, and bring upon us a disaster. Please show some gratefulness, so that we can enjoy this blessing."*

Once Jima finished her sentence a formidable noise came from the corridor. Both women panicked. Jima told Mandana to be quick and pick as many gems as she could. Mandana replied that it was difficult to carry more than a handful as they had no bags or anything else to stock up the trove. Jima looked down at her skirt and ripped two wide pieces of cloth. As she always dressed in the multi-layered fashion of women from the early 20th century, she could take off even more clothes and still remain decently covered. In a normal situation, Jima would have never done such a thing, as she was extremely careful with her belongings, but for the sake of the gems she might even have exposed her breasts.

Jima spread the two pieces of fabric and said:

"Here you are, let's put as many gems as possible in this skirt, and if we find any rings, earrings, bracelets or necklaces, we can wear them."

Mandana who had been frightened by the noise, promptly picked a few bunches of gems and dropped them on one of the skirts. She hurriedly donned some necklaces, bracelets and a huge diamond ring, and turned to Jima and said that she was ready to leave. Jima had her eyes on an adorned brooch and although she had already attached many things to her clothes, she fixed the precious piece to her shirt at the last minute and the two women ran down the corridor with their heavy packages. Mandana twisted the statue in order to open the access to the garden and they climbed up the stairs with such energy that they were back on the surface of the earth in no time.

Mandana looked at Jima and thought her eyes were deceiving her. Jima was covered head to foot in shiny ornaments – Mandana wasn't sure if she had ever witnessed a more ridiculous sight – a human Christmas tree in Kashmir. She told her aunt that somebody was bound to see them before they reached their rooms.

"If you are thinking of Farshid and his men, be assured that they are gone by now since the gods are now answering all our prayers," said Jima.

Mandana once again expressed her doubts about whether the gods even bothered with such petty requests:

"I really don't understand why the gods pay so much attention to us, when we have hardly done anything to deserve it. All this is too big a compensation for the little devotion you have demonstrated to them, and all I have done has been to challenge them."

"Listen, young lady, you have perhaps not lived long to understand how this world and its powers function. First of all, the gods follow a logic quite unlike ours, and it's impudent of you to even question why the gods should conform to your sense of just rewards. In your life you might encounter successful and happy people, and you might think that they have not worked hard for their success, but you don't know how much they have had to suffer to get what they have. Take my case, you don't know what I went through after the loss of my daughter.

My husband died shortly afterwards leaving me hardly any money. I have been humiliated all my life, having to depend financially on difficult people like Sima. Hardly anyone has shown me any affection or compassion. These precious stones are now going to give me some dignity. I will no longer need to beg here and there for money. I can have my own mansion, my own domestic help, my own social network."

"But your situation isn't unique. In a country like India where millions of people are starving, why would the gods choose you and me?"

"You ask too many questions," retorted Jima restlessly. *"The gods never asked us to understand them. All they expect from us is worship. Have you ever asked yourself why there is a sun and a moon, why there is a sky and a sea, why the dawn or dusk happen at a certain time of the day? All these happen for a reason or no reason. The gods don't seem to question it, and we shouldn't either. Some things would better remain unquestioned. Now please keep any other question of the kind to yourself before you bring a disaster upon us."*

Jima now had a hard time following Mandana's quick pace. She asked to sit down on a big stone which stood along their way to catch her breath. Mandana sat beside her and said:

"Despite your conviction that Farshid is gone, we still need to prepare ourselves for the worst. What shall we tell them if they see us with these bags and the jewels we are wearing?"

"I have enough of your questions and stupid worries," replied Jima in an exasperated tone, *"Why can't you have faith in the gods? There are people to whom the gods have never given anything and yet they believe in them with all their soul. You on the other hand have been offered half of the treasures of India and you still doubt their existence. Trust me, the gods have now taken Farshid back to Europe. I warn you, if you express any more doubts once again with regards to the gods, I will slap you, before the deities have any chance to punish you themselves."*

Mandana remained sceptical. She could not see any rationality in Jima's words. Nonetheless, she too now felt that she should no longer doubt the existence of the gods. She believed that they had done enough for them, and were now going to leave the two women to their own fate. She then thought to herself that the gods might have had a mission for them; otherwise, the whole business of giving away jewels made no sense.

While Mandana was deep in her thoughts, reflecting on how divine providence does or ought to operate, Jima said that they should come back another day, but much better equipped. Mandana was reluctant to do so. As she did not want Jima to lecture her once again about the gods, she decided to speak to Jima on her own terms:

"I don't know whether the gods would appreciate our taking more gems, as the gods disapprove of greedy people."

"What do you mean?" replied Jima. *"I need to take as many gems as possible in order to make extravagant purchases in front of Sima and Farshid. I need to buy my own palace in order to show them how wealthy I am."*

"Don't you think that the wealth the gods bestowed upon you could be used for a better purpose than showing off to your siblings? You are being ungrateful even to Sima, who offered you her hospitality. Talking about divine retribution, I think you are bound to experience it with your attitude. If you intent to go back to the well for more gems, you had better take a vow to open a big hostel for homeless people near here and dedicate your time looking after their well-being."

Jima looked at Mandana with horror:

"If I wanted to live such an abysmal life, why would I bother carrying heavy bags of jewels from one place to another?"

"Then you had better content yourself with what you have collected, and forget about the pit," advised the younger woman.

Jima did not expect such words from Mandana. Mandana's words were so powerful that they seemed to come from the mouth of a god. The last thing she wanted was to appear ungrateful before the divinities. She also had no intention of being mean; however, she was so obsessed with her siblings' wealth that she could not think of helping others.

Jima remained silent until they reached the palace. Both women looked at each other, and without much ado ran automatically to Jima's room, as it was the closest to the stairs. It was as if Jima herself had started doubting her own words, and was afraid to be perceived by Farshid.

"It would be difficult to hide these jewels for long, said Mandana, *"Chetra might find them when cleaning the room. I would recommend that we leave the country as soon as possible and sell these valuable through one of these auction houses."*

"How are we going to get a ticket? I have only a return ticket to Tehran," said Jima worriedly.

"Since the gods have been obliging until now, they have probably put some tickets under our pillows," replied Mandana in a sarcastic tone.

Jima dashed to look under her pillow, and instead of seeing a plane ticket, she heard what sounded like uproar from the skies. She turned to Mandana and said:

"The gods must be angry with us; we need to find a way to appease them."

Only Gems and No Money

Although Mandana believed that she owed the gods her newly acquired wealth, she was in no mood to hear their names once again. She wanted to find a way to Europe to sell the jewels. Her main challenge was to get them out of India. She was glad that she had at least her ticket back to France, but she did not know what to do with Jima. She asked Jima how much cash she had. Jima had only about three thousand rupees. This was far from being sufficient to purchase a ticket to Europe.

"*Didn't you sell your house in Tehran before coming?*" asked Mandana.

"*I didn't have time. The property market has suffered a lot due to the Revolution. It wasn't easy to find a buyer. I had half a million toman in the bank, with which I purchased gold Pahlavi coins. I brought them to India. I did not need more than four thousand rupees since I was sure that Sima would take care of most of my expenses here. I spent about a thousand rupees to get here from Delhi, so I should have some three thousand left.*"

Mandana looked in her own purse and tried to figure out how much money she had. She had about four thousand French francs, and a few Swiss coins.

"*I thought I had taken out seven thousand, but I must have spent a large proportion of it on some of those face creams.*"

"*You spent about three thousand francs on cosmetics!*" exclaimed Jima, "*Are you insane? You have not even hit thirty yet!*"

"*I was told that these ones are made with real pearl!*", as if that was a perfectly fitting response to an exasperated attempt by Jima to point out the absurdity of it.

"*Did you see somebody crush them in the container in front of you?*" asked Jima.

Mandana knew that she had squandered her money, but the saleswoman at the airport had been so convincing that Mandana could visualise her skin turning into satin after using these products. She could not find a sensible answer to her aunt's question; therefore, she led the conversation back to their initial subject, and noted that they had to find a way to pay for her flight to Europe:

"I guess we have no choice but to sell some of your gold coins once we get to Delhi. Let me call the airport and see if I can book us a flight today."

Saying this, Mandana went downstairs to make that call. An airport representative answered her call and explained to her that they had prepared a plane for three foreign gentlemen travelling to Delhi, and if they were able to reach the airport in an hour's time, they could go with them. Mandana asked the man whether it was 'Mr Gilipour' who had paid for the flight. The man was stunned and considered that Mandana may have possessed divinatory powers. Mandana was satisfied with his reply, and once again she did not know whether she should give into worshipping gods, or remain the sceptic that she was.

Mandana returned upstairs and told Jima to pack lightly and that they were going to travel by bus to Srinagar. Jima was appalled by the idea:

"Are you insane? I could never travel by bus. Only poor people do so. Why can't we fly to New Delhi?"

"There are no aircraft left. Farshid has taken the last one," replied Mandana.

"Just you wait and you will see the power and benevolence of the gods."

Mandana replied not without a hint of sarcasm:

"I can see their power, perhaps they can throw us a magic carpet too – that would sort out the travel issue."

Having said this, she dashed out of the room to avoid Jima's sermon on the gods again.

From her room, Mandana could hear Jima protesting that she did not intend to travel like a beggar. After packing her suitcase, Mandana went downstairs and asked Chetra how one could catch a bus to Srinagar. Chetra was stunned. She would have never thought that Ms Gilipour's relatives would be taking the bus to Srinigar. She told her that a coach to Srinagar left from the nearby village at seven o'clock in the morning once every two days, but then she - diplomatically, yet gingerly, as she didn't want to appear in any way judgemental of Jima, whom she struggled to see travelling by coach - suggested that perhaps her aunt might prefer to travel on a rickshaw. She even volunteered to book the rickshaw for them, as her cousin owned one. Mandana gladly accepted and asked Chetra if she could contact her cousin right away.

"It's difficult, as he doesn't have a phone," explained Chetra, *"but I can call a local grocer and ask him to find my cousin. When would you want him to come?"*

"As soon as possible," replied Mandana.

Mandana then went upstairs to let her aunt hear what she thought would be good news.

Upon hearing about Chetra's cousin and the rickshaw, Jima asked Mandana to thank the gods once again.

"Why shouldn't I thank Chetra instead?" asked Mandana.

"Because, though she doesn't seem to like us, she has offered to help us. This can be only the gods' doing."

Mandana did not see any point in arguing with the old woman. She finished packing and asked Jima to leave any unnecessary items behind.

As the two women were going downstairs, Chetra came to them and said that her cousin was going to be by the palace's gate in less than an hour. She added that he charged two hundred rupees to Srinagar. Mandana did not know much about drivers' wages in India, and hence accepted without any haggling. She was glad that at least there was somebody to take them to the other side of the province.

An Endless Trip

The two Iranian women were so anxious not to be in short supply of water and food that they overstocked their picnic baskets. The journey from *Ganjbaran* to Srinagar, they were told, would take more than five hours. Mandana was planning to take a kip in the rickshaw, not realising how uncomfortable the seats would be. Jima was imagining the long drawn sermons she would now be able to force on Mandana during their rickshaw journey with a view to making her a devout and god-fearing lady.

Chetra and the driver put two big handbags and two small suitcases in the rickshaw along with two big baskets of food and water. There was barely enough space for Jima and Mandana to stretch their legs. Mandana's hopes of sleeping were shattered. As the two women thanked Chetra and bid her farewell, Jima commenced with her discourse on the gods, and the driver started the rickshaw.

Mandana, who could no longer bear hearing the name of a single god, said to Jima:

"Jima is it because you have not had a man in your life since the death of your husband, or because you have not had a great social life, that you have taken refuge in the divine?"

"If you had some faith in the gods," retorted Jima in a disconcerted tone, *"you might have thought less of just having a man. I could see that you have had no mother to bring you up."*

Neither of the women now desired to speak to the other. Mandana was so tired and bored that, despite her uncomfortable seat, she fell asleep.

About six hours later, the rickshaw arrived in Srinagar. Mandana woke up extremely hungry. Jima had already eaten her meal and drunk more than a litre of lemonade. She was now desperate to find a water closet. The driver wished to know where the two women planned to get off. Mandana asked the driver to drop them by an office where they could purchase plane or train tickets to New Delhi. Jima objected, she needed to be dropped at a guesthouse, where she could get some rest and use the facilities. Seeing how desperate Jima looked, Mandana did not object. The rickshaw driver stopped on four occasions to ask for directions to a guesthouse. The fifth person was finally able to give them an address, as he worked in a guesthouse himself.

Once at the guesthouse, Mandana asked the driver to wait as she wanted him to take her to a train ticket stall. Mandana and Jima had a hard time communicating with the person working at the guesthouse. After lots of gestures and exchanges of words incomprehensible to both parties, the two women were finally ushered to a big room which was decorated with cheap furniture and dirty curtains. Both women disapproved of it and insisted on seeing another room, but the second and third rooms were much the same, if not worse. Mandana told Jima to accept the first room and use its bathroom, while she went to book a ticket. She said if they were lucky, they could leave that day and be in New Delhi perhaps the following morning.

When Mandana returned, Jima was lying on the bed. She had covered the pillow with one of her own blouses, as she had misgivings about the hygiene of the guesthouse. Mandana could hear the tap in the bathroom dripping.

"*At what time are we leaving this place?*" Jima enquired.

"*Early tomorrow morning.*"

"*This is impossible,*" objected Jima. "*I couldn't possibly spend the night in this hole. Why couldn't you get us out of here today?*"

"*I did my best. I even had to bribe the salesman to get us a first class ticket to Delhi.*"

"*I would rather leave today in second class, than tomorrow in first class,*" replied Jima.

"*You probably don't know how bad Indian trains can get on second class,*" said Mandana.

Jima, obviously shocked at this piece of information shouted at her niece:

"You mean we are travelling by train tomorrow? I thought that you meant first class by plane. No wonder you have not been to university – it's because they wouldn't have had you - you are incapable of even booking a flight to Delhi."

The two women quarrelled until Jima said that she was thirsty and that they needed to find a store where they could purchase some bottled water. While searching for a shop, they passed by a food stall selling bread baked on the spot. Jima asked Mandana to purchase a few loaves of bread as she said she could not see herself eating anything else that day, since she could not trust the hygiene of the eateries of the city. Mandana and Jima ended their exploration of Srinagar by purchasing some hand woven Kashmiri shawls with embroideries. Once back to the guesthouse it was already dark. Jima changed quickly and went to bed in order to disconnect from her surroundings as soon as she could.

A Seduced Man

The following morning, Mandana and Jima took the train to New Delhi. After twelve hours they reached the capital of India. Mandana told Jima that they would probably have to stay in a hotel for another night before leaving for Europe. However, instead of worrying about the standard of the hotels in New Delhi, they had to worry about their cost; for Delhi indeed had luxurious hotels, and they had plenty of choices. Once at the hotel, Mandana said:

"*While I inquire about flights to France, go to the French embassy and see if you can sort out the visa situation.*"

Mandana was quite disoriented. She decided to look for an *Alliance Francaise*, or a British Council branch and see if they could recommend an efficient travel agency. She incidentally saw a Swissair agency and went in. The doorman was extremely unpleasant and so were the agents. Nobody wanted to assist her. She asked to see the manager, telling the agents that she worked at the Swiss embassy and needed to discuss something important. The manager came out of one of the offices, intrigued. He was a Swiss man in his mid-forties, and could tell right away by looking at Mandana that she was neither Swiss, nor local.

Mandana went forward with a smile and introduced herself: "*Bonjour, Mandana Gilipour*", and shook hands with the manager. The man did not know what to make of it, but was interested to know who this strange young woman was, and what she wanted. Since she was beautiful and elegantly dressed, and a foreigner, he felt comfortable with introducing himself and inviting her to his office:

"*Maxime Teller, please allow me to offer you some refreshments in my office.*"

Since Mandana had greeted Maxime with a *bonjour*, he continued the conversation in French. Once in the office he asked Mandana what she wished to drink. Mandana gladly asked for a cup of tea. Then Maxime asked:

"So, I was told that you work at the Swiss embassy. I must tell you that I frequently visit the embassy and not once have I had the pleasure of meeting you."

"I was born in Switzerland," answered Mandana. *"I just arrived in New Delhi from Kashmir and am completely lost. I don't know how to find my way to a travel agency as I need to get back to Europe. When I saw Swissair, I was relieved and thought that I could at least get some help and advice."*

"But you don't seem to have a Swiss accent," Maxime ventured to remark.

"That is because I grew up in the south of France."

"And what are you doing in Kashmir?"

"I am visiting my aunt."

"In Kashmir!" exclaimed the Swissair manager in disbelief.

Mandana was not pleased with the man's reaction. She got up and said:

"Listen, I did not come here to be interrogated. It seems that you want to waste my time."

Maxime laughed and asked: *"Mandana, what is exactly the purpose of your coming here? If it were only to purchase tickets, you could have done so by speaking to one of my employees at the front desk."*

"I am planning to travel with my aunt to Europe and she doesn't have any money. I need to sell my aunt's gold coins in order to purchase a ticket. I need to find an honest jeweller. I thought you could help me."

Mandana's innocence softened Maxime, who laughed again and said:

"Honesty and jewel business don't go together. However, I can still introduce you to a Swiss friend of mine who is a jeweller and is currently in India. So I presume this is the same aunt that you have been visiting in Kashmir. Was she trapped in Kashmir without any money? You should really love this aunt of yours in order to be so concerned about her well-being."

Mandana realised that there was no point in giving detailed explanations, since he was not going to believe her. She just said: *"Yes."* The manager did not believe the story that he had tried to reconstruct himself. However, he was intrigued, and perhaps, rather seduced by Mandana. He asked her to sit down while he went to call his friend, and then invited Mandana to have lunch with him.

A Closed Gate

While Mandana was busy at seducing a man, Jima had managed to enter the French embassy. She had fought with the rickshaw driver who had driven her there and had refused to pay the exaggerated fare he had asked. He had mistaken Jima for a fragile foreign old woman and was surprised to see an assertive shrewd person whom he could not swindle.

At the embassy, Jima had adamantly requested to speak to the ambassador, and her request had been flatly rejected. The staff was very rude to the poor Iranian woman. They insulted her both in French and English with the most unimaginably indecent words, and took her passport and stamped on it "*en aucun cas un visa devrait être délivré à cet individu*" (under no circumstances shall a visa be issued to this person). Then Security was called to take Jima away. Two Indian men came to take Jima, however, the old lady pulled herself away from them. The poor men did not know what to do, and did not have the heart to drag Jima out.

A young French man came, saying loud to his colleagues, "*ces imbéciles d'Indiens ne peuvent même pas foutre dehors une Arabe.*" He went towards Jima, and pulled her arm in such a way that Jima thought she had lost it for good. He opened the door of the embassy and threw the poor old woman out on the floor of the courtyard. The two Indian security men, went out and helped Jima get up, and asked her if she was able to walk. Jima was hurt both physically and emotionally, and began to cry. The two men decided to ask one of the drivers of the embassy to accompany Jima to her hotel. As the driver was their friend he accepted.

In the car, Jima inquired if everyone in New Delhi was this kind.

"No," responded the driver. "*My friend and I are from Lucknow. You should watch out in Delhi.*"

Once at the hotel, the driver got out, opened the door for Jima and accompanied her all the way up the stairs to the entrance and told the doorman that Jima was injured and had to be taken to her room. Jima thanked the driver, and insisted in tipping him ten rupees but he refused.

Jima went up to her room, and lied on the bed in reflective distress. It was now clear that she could not travel to Europe with Mandana. She had no visa. She was impatiently waiting for Mandana to return.

The Key to a Successful Business

Maxime tried every possible way he could think of to take Mandana to his flat. Mandana insisted that she would go to his place only after meeting the jeweller and negotiating with him the price of the gold coins. Maxime offered to give Mandana two first class seats to France provided she would reconsider her plans for the day. Mandana adamantly said that she needed to meet the gem dealer. Once at the dealer's, she requested to call her aunt and speak to her. Jima gave her the bad news, and therefore, their plan to sell the jewels in Europe was no longer tenable. Mandana had to find a way now to sell all the jewels in Delhi. If she showed all the jewels and sold them there, she knew she could hardly get the desired amount.

Mandana wished to find a more reputable gem dealer, but for the time being she had no choice but to negotiate with this one, as she had to pay the hotel bills. She was now a bit anxious that the gold coins would not suffice to pay for the hotel bills if they had to stay longer in New Delhi. She decided to show the dealer the necklace she was wearing under her shirt. This was the simplest jewellery they had found in the pit, and despite its simplicity she was still able to impress the gem dealer. The dealer unconvincingly feigned to be uninterested, but his astonished eyes belied appearances since the necklace was quite unusual. He was curious to know how Mandana had come to possess it. Mandana told him that it had been in her family for generations.

The dealer clearly intended to make the lowest offer possible, but he was conscious that the necklace was old and was made of a string of rubies. He offered Mandana four thousand dollars, which Mandana refused outright. Her intuition told her that he was offering her a fraction of what the necklace was worth. The dealer gradually increased his offer but refused to budge above eight thousand. Mandana was genuinely offended and decided to walk away. Maxime wished to intervene as he did not want to lose Mandana. As Mandana opened the door, the dealer asked Mandana to state her asking price. Mandana said that she would not sell the necklace for less than fourteen thousand dollars as it was a collectible object. The deal was sealed at twelve thousand.

"*As our mission has been accomplished,*" said Maxime, "*may I invite you for lunch?*"

"*You may invite me, my aunt and the dealer for lunch, as my mission isn't completely finished.*"

The airline manager was not expecting such a reply. As he still had hope of having Mandana, he accepted to invite all of them to a restaurant at a five-star hotel called, quite appositely, the *Koh-e Noor*.

The gem dealer took Mandana and Maxime to his bank to get dollar notes, and once their business was finished they went to fetch Jima. Meanwhile, Jima had had her nap and was waiting impatiently for Mandana to return. Once Mandana entered the room, Jima opened her mouth to shower her with questions. Mandana did not give her the chance to speak. She told her aunt to hurry and find a hiding place for the money and follow her downstairs:

"*There are two men waiting for us, one is a gem dealer and the other one an airline manager. The latter has invited us for lunch as he thinks that I will be sleeping with him. We need to take advantage of the momentum and push them to find us a dealer capable of purchasing the larger stones. I have a feeling that the one who is accompanying me has not the means to buy any jewel worth more than twenty or thirty thousand dollars.*"

The Ever Hospitable Palace

The Ever Hospitable Palace *Ganjbaran* now had no one left but Chetra. But even she was preparing to leave. She tidied the kitchen in such a way that no harmful insect would invade it during everyone's absence. Chetra sealed all the bags of beans, rice, salt and sugar, and placed them in the cupboards. She then packed all the food likely to turn stale or rancid, and called the shopkeeper of her village to locate her cousin and send him to *Ganjbaran*. Her cousin arrived and she left the palace, locking all the doors and windows.

Ganjbaran seemed even more extraordinary without human presence. Although cold days were approaching, the tree leaves at *Ganjbaran* were still as green as ever. Flowers still covered the gardens; birds were still singing on the trees. Small rabbits, pheasants, chirus and deers strolled on the lawn. The lotuses that adorned the basins and the pools remained open. The palace seemed so tranquil and was within an ace of becoming a paradise, when three old cars turned up.

Sima got out of one of the cars and ran to the door of the palace but the door was closed and locked. All those who had accompanied her came out of the vehicles. Mona, seeing Sima puzzled, asked her what was wrong. Sima said that nobody was in the palace and that she wondered where Jima and Mandana had gone. A man with the appearance of a fashion model got out of the car and came up the stairs and asked whether the palace had a secret entrance. Sima replied:

"*Karl, you have been reading too many stories.*"

Then, a little woman jumped beside them and asked:

"*Do only Jima and Mandana have the keys?*"

"*No Azar dear,*" replied Sima. "*Chetra, my housekeeper, has one too and she is probably gone to the village. We must go and fetch her.*"

Azar did not let a second pass by and called her boys:

"*Pedram! Rambod! Accompany Sima to the village!*"

Two short yet athletic teenagers jumped in the car with Sima and were driven off to the village.

After two hours Sima, Pedram and Rambod were back with Chetra. Two other servants were to come later in the day. Chetra walked ahead and opened the main door to let everyone in.

"*According to my housekeeper,*" said Sima, "*Jima and Mandana have left for Delhi.*"

Azar who was one of the nosiest members of the family, inquired:

"*Why would they suddenly decide to go to Delhi?*"

And aghast by the beauty of *Ganjbaran*, she did not wait for Sima's answer and complimented her on her taste. Karl, who was not standing very far, added that it was how he imagined paradise to be. Azar's husband, Bahram, praised Sima's spring for its freshness.

Half an hour later the whole family had gathered in the main living room. Azar turned to Sima and Mona, and continued with her queries:

"*Has Jima now moved to India for good? Does she have enough money to survive by herself or is she entirely dependent on you?*"

"*I am really not aware of my sister's financial situation.*"

Azar then looked at Mona, who gave her a similar answer. They both felt uncomfortable telling Azar that a person so close to them was badly off. Realising that both women did not approve of her question, Azar changed the subject, and made a statement which she hoped would satisfy her curiosity:

"*I never really got to find out what Farshid had done to Mandana's mother.*"

Farshid had apparently turned his ex-wife's life to sheer hell. Although Sima did not like her brother, she thought that to discredit him would be disgraceful to her own family. Moreover, whatever Azar had been told, Sima thought, became common knowledge - at the most Antartica's daily may have missed reporting on it. Azar was smart enough to understand that her questions were making others uncomfortable and had annoyed Sima. She turned instead to Mona and asked her where she thought her mother had gone. Mona was no longer listening to Azar. She was so happy to have Karl near her that she really did not care whether her mother was dead or alive. Sima was as curious as Azar to know why her sister and niece had left, but knew perfectly that no one in *Ganjbaran* knew the answer.

GEMS FOR THE PURSES OF ARABIA

In the meantime, while Sima and Azar were standing clueless in *Ganjbaran*, Jima and Mandana had made the acquaintance of a number of gem dealers, some of whom were working for renowned jewellers in Europe. Maxime's friend had contacted them for the two Iranian women. Since they had not been able to make their way to Europe to sell their gems in an auction, Maxime had thought his friends could find for them a solution. Jima and Mandana knew that their jewels would be valued less in India than in Europe, and therefore, still hoped for a better alternative.

While Jima and Mandana were distressed about the idea of selling their gems at a discount, Sebastian, one of the gem dealers, wanted to impress Mandana. He bragged about his connection to Arab royal households and the Sultan of Brunei. Maxime could not bear Sebastian, as he was convinced that Mandana preferred Sebastian's company because he was ten years younger than him.

Mandana looked at both of her admirers, and was struck by an idea. She asked Sebastian if he could introduce her to one of the Arab sheikhs, and mention to him that he should not miss the deal that Mandana was offering him. She then asked Maxime if he could book two seats for her and Jima to whatever city in the Persian Gulf proposed by Sebastian. Maxime proposed to offer them free first class tickets on the condition that he could travel with them too. Mandana could not expect anything better. With two men after her she would be attended to as if she were a queen. Both would be competing for her regard, and she need not give them anything in exchange, other than sustain enough of their interest until her plan came to its conclusion.

Sebastian made a few calls, and then announced that he had secured an appointment with one of the brothers of Kuwait's crown prince. Mandana then asked Sebastian if he could ask the prince to arrange for Jima's visa otherwise their meeting would not materialise. A driver was sent to pick up Jima's passport, the plane tickets were booked, and they were all bound to leave in less than 24 hours. Mandana's beauty and voluptuousness had had the desired effect on these poor men.

The following day, Jima's passport was returned with a Kuwaiti visa, and since both Sebastian and Maxime knew people at the airport, Mandana and Jima managed to pass seamlessly through the customs with their precious jewels.

Once aboard, Jima told Mandana:

"Even when the French threw me out of their embassy, I still knew that the gods had not abandoned us. Look at our blessings now. Had we gone alone to Europe as originally planned, our bags might have been searched by Indian customs officers, and we might have lost every hope of riches; we might have had to travel in second class, and we might not have found the right dealers either. I have heard so many horror stories of gems and antiques being stolen in auction houses in France before the actual auctions had taken place. I trust the Arabs much more than the French when it comes to money. I am sure we are going to strike a better deal with the prince in Kuwait. The gods have really arranged everything for us."

"The gods!" exclaimed Mandana in an irriated tone. *"Instead of thanking me for all my efforts, you mention the gods? While you were lying on the bed at the hotel, I was negotiating hard with these men to get us here. Seducing men isn't an easy task, especially when you don't want to sleep with them, and need their assistance. I advise you not to mention the name of the gods in Kuwait; since you are Iranian they probably expect you to be Muslim, or at least fit in one of these Abrahamic religions. Mention your gods over there and you will see how we are going to lose our deal."*

Unaffected by her niece's words, Jima said:

"Even in Kuwait city, the gods are going to be with us, whether I mention their name or not. These people don't intimidate me."

Sebastian, who was not sitting far from the two women, commented:

"*It is a shame that you ladies are too involved in your passionate exchange to enjoy the cocktails.*"

Mandana replied in a sensual voice:

"*You are so right Sebastian, my aunt and I are all yours now.*"

The prospect of Jima being in any way his, or anywhere in his proximity, did not delight him in the slightest, and he feigned a smile to express genuine gratitude for Mandana's response.

INCOMPREHENSIBLE SENTIMENTS

Sima was walking restlessly in her garden. Although she generally enjoyed her crowded family, this time they were exhausting her: Mona, because of her problems with Karl; and Jima and Mandana because of their secretive schemes. Although she knew that Mona was not in a happy marriage, she could not help envying her for having a handsome and vigorous husband. She herself had been involved in many relationships, but none of them had been passionate. None of the men to whom she was attracted courted her or expressed any desire to marry her. There had been two men in particular she had coveted. One came from a wealthy Iranian family and was a Cambridge graduate seeking work experience in New York. He was going back to Iran to run his family business. He was also very attractive, with shiny black hair and immaculate white teeth. Sima hoped to become pregnant by him, so that the young man would then feel obliged to marry her. Unfortunately for her, he was too intelligent and cautious to fall into her trap. Then she targeted another young man, this time of Indian origin, as handsome as a Bollywood star, not as wealthy as the previous one, but again with very good prospects. He had just obtained his law degree from a renowned American university, and was offered a job at a reputable firm shortly after Sima had met him. No matter how much Sima tried to impress him with her temporary involvement in politics, taking piano lessons and perusing the Kama Sutra to its infinite detail, her wealthy handsome lawyer slipped out of her hands like an eel.

And now Mona and Karl were in front of her, bringing back all these memories, and reminding her of her sentimental failures. How could Mona, with no beauty, no charm and no skills, have secured herself a partner like Karl, while she, with all her professional success, had no one? Had she given up too soon? After her Indian lover left her for another woman, she was so hurt that she wanted to prove to him that he had missed the chance of his lifetime. She focused on her career, and only dated men who did not mean anything to her, but were means to her ends. Now, she was only too acutely aware that her pursuit of a career and her strife to amass a fortune had led to her underinvesting in human relationships, and consequently, she was left with a family who did little to show her any affection but who clung to her for financial support.

Sima had been through too many ups and downs to allow this realisation and the tide of regret it occasioned to bring her down – no point crying over spilt milk, she thought, though this in no way lessened the sober mood that her reflection had caused, nor did it negate whatever she had in hindsight concluded from this. She had this fantastic ability to look at the positive aspects of her life and weigh her luck against that of other people. At this point she decided to look at Mona's situation with lucidity. She saw an unattractive woman in love with a successful man who was and would remain unfaithful to her. Mona had invested neither in a career nor in friends and family. She had nothing else but Karl, and was bound to suffer throughout her life until her husband became impotent and stayed at home.

Azar and Bahram seemed happily married, but they were an average couple who had spent all their lives working and filling the coffers of the government. Although Azar had no university education or special skills, she had to work along with her husband in order to make ends meet. She worked as a salesperson in a clothing shop, and then in the evenings, she attended to the needs of her husband and children. On weekends she cleaned her home, and during the week she did the cooking and shopping, without ever asking herself whether she enjoyed these tasks or not. Bahram was a rather boring husband with whom she had no interesting conversations, and who had few friends of his own. The couples Azar befriended, became his friends as well. Sima found that sort of existence unbearable.

Sima then realised that she had been walking for too long, and dinner was to be served soon. Once back at the palace she saw that Azar was in the kitchen helping Chetra with the cooking. She was so much used to doing domestic chores that she struggled simply to rest along with Mona and the men, or simply enjoy herself. Sima entered the kitchen to give the final touches to the dishes and make everyone else believe that she was indeed the capable cook that churned out these delicacies. She added rose water to the rice draining in the colander, an act which appeared like profanity to Azar. Sima then pushed aside Chetra, who was about to pour the rice on a serving dish, and said as if she were giving a cooking lesson:

"*Rice is fragile, you should be very careful with the way you wash it or serve it.*"

Azar was not impressed with the untimely cooking lessons, but let her cousin perform at her leisure. Soon after, an Indo-Iranian table was set with a variety of rice, some mixed with dried nuts and raisins, some with dried berries, and some plain, but all spiced with Kashmiri saffron. Five lamb and chicken dishes *à l'iranienne* and *à l'indienne* mixed with a variety of vegetables were also on the menu. Fresh baskets of mixed herbs, such as basil, tarragon, mint, coriander, and radish were placed at each corner of the table. Chetra had also baked the Iranian guests some *naan* bread.

While Mona, Azar, their husbands and their children were talking quite animatedly and enjoying their meal, Sima remained pensive and ate without saying much. Azar turned to her and asked in a concerned tone:

"*What is the matter?*"

Sima could not tell her that she was not in a mood to talk, she simply answered that she was worried about Jima and Mandana.

The Gold-Digger's Marriage Proposal

In Kuwait, Mandana had managed to meet with the prince and one of his treasurers without Sebastian. Sebastian had tried hard to convince Mandana to let him negotiate for her, as he was hoping somehow to benefit from their transaction, but Mandana used all her charm to let him down gently with regard to his aspirations to enrich himself. Since he had not seen Mandana's gems, he conceded, as he did not know how much money was at stake.

Jima and Mandana took out of silk purses the larger gems in their hands and displayed them before the two Arab men. They were enthralled. They had been expecting to see some sort of old Persian or Indian jewellery, but nothing that could compete in splendour with their crown jewels. They wanted both women to wait a couple of weeks so that they could have the gems valued, but Mandana tried to entice them to an instant sale by suggesting that they would get a deal if they bought there and then. She argued that she had to return to India immediately to purchase a palace, and that if she failed to have the money in time she was going to lose it to another purchaser.

The prince had asked Mandana for her price, but she had difficulty thinking of a figure. She just knew that the big diamonds in the Iranian and British crown jewels were considered invaluable, on a separate par altogether, and would certainly not sell for anything less than several hundred million. Her rubies and emeralds were as big, and her diamonds not much smaller. Mandana just mentioned to the prince that with these gems she was offering him the opportunity to create a collection surpassing other known collection of crown jewels.

The prince conceded that the gems appeared priceless, but his treasurer interfered and said that His Highness could not offer anything exceeding thirty million pounds.

Mandana and Jima took more gems out of their purses and negotiated an additional five million, a hefty sum in 1979. The two ladies were ushered to a bank in Kuwait and an account was opened for them on the spot. Thirty-five million pounds were then transferred in their favour, and Mandana and Jima separated their accounts right away.

On their way back to India, the two women did not know whether they were flying on a plane or whether it was an extended joint flight of their imaginations – they thought, the mind does play tricks sometimes on consciousness, but although plausible this was too extensive, too complicated, and too sustained to be something of the sort. Sebastian had received five gold coins from the prince for bringing him such precious guests. Maxime was doing his best to attend to the two ladies, and was becoming more and more obsessed with Mandana. Five minutes before the plane landed, Sebastian gathered all his courage and proposed to Mandana. Jima did not allow a second to pass; she was afraid that Sebastian had discovered something about the amount they had received, and therefore responded instead of her niece:

"Young man, the prince just proposed before you, and Mandana turned him down. She is looking for a really exceptional person, you know."

Sebastian did not let this dampen his spirits, however, as he was quite convinced by now that Jima was very idiosyncratic and particular with regard to her mental faculties. He just looked at Mandana who in response laughed seductively, spurring him on.

A Precious Advice

Both Sebastian and Maxime inquired how long the two ladies were planning to stay in New Delhi. Mandana replied that she needed to return to *Ganjbaran* immediately. Both men were disappointed and begged Mandana to stay. Maxime knew that unless he used his contacts, Mandana and Jima could not leave the same day for Kashmir. He told Mandana that unless he was allowed to accompany them to *Ganjbaran*, he would not book the plane for them. Sebastian insisted that he wished to visit the region also. Maxime wanted to strangle Sebastian, as he felt that he had taken away his chance of having Mandana as mistress.

"*I don't have any objections to your accompanying us,*" said Mandana, "*however, Ganjbaran isn't a resort; it's my aunt's residence. She wouldn't be pleased to see two male strangers accompanying her niece and planning to stay overnight.*"

Maxime turned to Jima and asked:

"*Madame, can we possibly accompany you to your palace.*"

"*Ganjbaran doesn't belong to this aunt of mine, but another one,*" replied Mandana.

"*You could take me along then and introduce me as your fiancé,*" said Sebastian, "*and say that you want her to meet me.*"

This only made Maxime erupt and a fist fight ensued between him and Sebastian which Mandana managed to bring to a close by reminding both men that altercations at airports are not taken lightly by airport security.

Jima had enough of the two men. As their assistance was no longer vital, she intervened and told the men that neither of them was accompanying them to Kashmir. She then turned to Maxime and said:

"If you are not going to help us find a flight this afternoon, we will manage without you and leave tomorrow."

Anxious not to alienate both men before she was truly no longer in need of them, Mandana apologised to them for her aunt's rather prickly reaction, and said in an almost flirtatious yet apologetic, tone that her aunt was tired and could not bear further negotiations. She promised to invite both men to *Ganjbaran*, and gave them the palace's phone number. Maxime booked a plane to the airport nearest to *Ganjbaran*. Mandana hugged and kissed both men, while Jima went off without bidding them farewell.

On the plane, Jima asked Mandana what she planned to do in the coming months. Mandana could not help smiling, as the future seemed to her brighter than ever. Not only had she achieved the financial independence she had been yearning for all these years, she had also received a marriage proposal. She pithily responded to Jima:

"Perhaps, get married and move to some nice warm island."

"Why didn't I guess so?" said Jima, *"Most young beautiful wealthy women can hardly think with their brain when it comes to men. And you are probably going to take Sebastian as your lawful husband…?"*

Mandana tried to interrupt Jima, but she did not let her.

"Listen to me Mandana. You might think that I am an old cranky woman, but I have lived many decades more than you; I have my experiences behind me. I might not have dated an army, like women do these days, but I have seen hundreds of people get entangled in relationships, lose their head and money, and end with a broken heart. You have now too much at stake. You can't run away with the first man appearing on the scene."

"Are you referring to Sebastian?"

"Yes indeed," continued Jima. *"The only thing he knows about you, is that you are a beautiful and wealthy woman - nothing more. He is also a gem dealer, which should already tell you that he is probably untrustworthy. In addition, you don't know what kind of a family he comes from, what type of education he has had and what has been his past."*

"Since he is a gem dealer, he can't be poor himself," replied Mandana.

"Yes, but that also means that he runs desperately after money, and he can never be satisfied," retorted Jima. *"Since the women's emancipation movement has*

taken place, take the time to date men, learn to know them, introduce them to your friends and family - see if they fit in your world. These points might seem futile when one is attracted to someone, but they are extremely important. I have seen Sebastian, and I can already safely say that he appears worthless. Even the airline manager, despite his age was more suitable."

In order to put an end to the conversation, Mandana said:

"You should worry about me, were I planning to marry Sebastian."

Not long afterwards, the two women were driven back to *Ganjbaran*. It was nearly midnight, and everybody, other than Bahram and Karl, was asleep. These two were still awake discussing life and wife. Karl was pouring himself some banana liquor when Bahram decided he was tired and should head towards his bedroom. Karl did not feel like sleeping, his gaze fell on a bookshelf in the drawing room. He randomly picked up a book, which happened to be on Indo-Iranian mythology. He then heard the voice of two women whispering to each other. He thought that Sima and Azar had come back downstairs. Then he saw a woman entering the drawing room. He recognized Mandana immediately, recalling her face from the pictures he had seen; her beauty had not left him indifferent. It was lust at first sight. Mandana forgot all about Sebastian and Karl forgot his mistresses:

"You must be the famous Mandana!"

"And you the infamous Karl!" said Mandana, both laughing.

Karl offered Mandana a glass of banana liquor and indeed not only Sebastian, but the entire world was forgotten.

THE TZARINE IN PERSON

The next morning the whole family other than Karl and Mandana gathered at the breakfast table. They were all surprised to see Jima sitting in front of them, and the men of the family were even more so to see a woman dressed in nineteenth century European attire. Since she was wearing a brooch she had found in the pit, she felt superior to everybody else in the room, as if she were the Tzarina of all Russia. The brooch consisted of a big emerald surrounded by small diamonds and topped by a big pearl and golden feathers. Rambod and Pedram had already decided that she was insane. Sima was slightly agitated. She knew Jima had been up to something, and she knew that she would not be able to get the truth out of her. Azar on the other hand was more confident in her interrogation skills, and led the conversation:

"It's so wonderful, Jima, to see you. We were all wondering where you had been. The idea of having two of our female relatives travelling by themselves in India did worry us. Tell us about your trip."

Jima saw that for the first time in years everybody's attention was drawn towards her. She could not lose the momentum. Delighted she began narrating her story:

"We were a bit bored in the palace. There wasn't much to be done except to walk in the garden and drink tea. We thought that it would be a pity to have come all the way to India and miss out on sightseeing. I was dying to see the Taj Mahal, and Mandana the Lotus Temple."

Sima interrupted her:

"Why of all the places would Mandana want to see the Lotus Temple? Has she developed an interest in new religions or modern architecture?"

Jima did not pay any heed to Sima and continued:

"*On our way to Agra, a young Swiss gentleman fell in love with me and decided to accompany us and take care of all our expenses. He owned Swissair.*"

Azar suddenly noticed Jima's brooch. She interrupted her and asked:

"*Did you purchase this gem in Delhi?*"

In front of strangers Jima always bragged about the wealth of her family, and was about to say that she had got it from her mother, but suddenly she realised that her sister was nearby and said:

"*I did not purchase anything during this trip. This young man did not let us. He was completely enamoured of me. He asked for my hand and offered me this brooch. At my age I couldn't possibly remarry. In my mind I am still married to my late husband. I accepted the brooch and rejected his hand.*"

While Jima was narrating her story, Bahram whispered in his wife's ear that he had heard enough rubbish and wanted to explore the gardens of the palace with his sons. He turned to his sons and told them to finish quickly their breakfast and go along to see the botanical treasures of Kashmir. He then turned to Jima and apologised and left. Jima was not happy to lose a part of her audience, but at the same time she could see that Sima was losing her patience and did not want to be left alone with her. She suddenly turned to Pedram and said:

"*My beautiful son, before you leave could you bring me a glass of mandarin juice from the kitchen? Chetra will tell you where to find some.*"

Pedram got up irritated and mumbled to himself some nasty words about Jima and went to the kitchen. Sima turned to Azar and said:

"*I am really sorry Azar, the older generation in our family has always confused children with servants.*"

Jima was not pleased with Sima's statement, and told her that there was nothing wrong in her requesting the young boy to get a glass of mandarin juice:

"*The servants were not within calling distance and I did not want to trouble you or Azar.*"

"*My dear sister, you could have perfectly well gone to the kitchen yourself.*"

Shortly after, a quarrel ensued. Azar and Mona took advantage of it to leave and go for a walk with their children in the garden.

YEARNING FOR LOVE

Sima could not have asked for a better opportunity to cross-examine her sister:

"You have said enough nonsense for the day. Why would you want to make a fool of yourself and your sister? Do you think people buy your lies? A young man owning Swissair fell in love with you and asked for your hand? Are you senile? Where did you get this brooch from? I could tell that it isn't fake."

Just then Mandana entered the room. Having heard Sima's sentences she said:

"Jima's stories were not complete lies, I believe she just substituted me with herself. Indeed, a Swiss man fell in love with me, and gave me this brooch, he also asked for my hand. I wouldn't say however that he was young."

Sima could still not believe the story. The brooch was too rare and valuable. Her intuition was telling her that they had found it somewhere in her palace, and she should have become the rightful owner of it. She glared at the two women for ten seconds and left.

Mandana turned to Jima and asked her why she had put that brooch on?

"Couldn't you have chosen a more discreet piece of jewellery? And why did you have to tell such an unbelievable story, so as to arouse Sima's suspicion? In addition, Sebastian isn't Swiss. If at any point he calls me here and Sima answers, she is definitely going to invite him to see whether what we have said is true. We told him that these were family jewels and we now told Sima that a Swiss suitor gave me the brooch."

Mandana then went on the porch with an apple in her hand. While she was crunching away, she saw from afar Mona and her children walking side by side. She then remembered Karl's kiss last night, and her mind flew away. She suddenly had a desire to be married and have children of her own. She was anxious that she might never marry. She did not know how to find the right man. She believed her situation was different from that of the other women in her family. They had all had a chance to meet eligible men in different receptions held by elder relatives. The future husbands were all from the same milieu as the girls. The parents knew their background.

After the Iranian revolution all this had changed. Outside Iran there were no more extravagant evenings which Mandana could attend. Being a foreigner, she was marginalized and not invited to such events. Her only hope was that the older members of the family would remember to introduce her to young men of her status. But the revolution had given Iranians such a shock that matchmaking was really their last concern. Mandana thus had no choice but to find her own way. Beautiful as she was, she had no problem meeting young men; however, the men she met were not really meant for her. The majority were not sophisticated like her. Almost any young man she encountered had a serious flaw: if he came from a well-established family, he had no university education and no employment prospects. If he was educated, he did not have the means to offer the comfort with which she was brought up. Mandana did not want her future spouse to live off her father's or her own newly acquired money.

Another factor which had prevented Mandana from choosing a husband was the importance she gave to appearance. She failed to find most men she had encountered even remotely physically attractive. She wondered how she could find a man like Karl: handsome, athletic, from a reputed family, not to mention educated and professional. While she was thinking of Karl, he appeared behind her and wanted to kiss her on the neck. Mandana stopped him instinctively telling him that his wife could see them from afar and that it was inappropriate.

"Then we should go somewhere far from anyone's sight," replied Karl.

Mandana initially objected but gave in to Karl's insistence. She felt that what she was doing was morally wrong, but she truly desired Karl and wanted to be held in his arms.

THE PERSEVERANT SUITOR

While Mandana had run off behind the bushes with Karl, the telephone rang. Sima answered. It was Sebastian calling from New Delhi and wishing to speak to Mandana. Sima was aghast. She could not believe that Mandana's story was indeed true:

"You mentioned that your name was Sebastian. My niece had mentioned meeting a Swiss gentleman, but I did not think that it was very serious. So, are your intentions honourable?"

Sebastian objected to being thought of as 'Swiss' but didn't deny that he wished to ask for Mandana's hand. He said he wished to visit *Ganjbaran*, but he knew that there were no hotels in the vicinity where he could stay. Sima was so curious to see him and hear his version of the story of the brooch that she did not hesitate one second to invite him to stay overnight at *Ganjbaran*. Sebastian was over the moon. He said that he would be in *Ganjbaran* later in the evening. Thus, Mandana's prediction materialised.

The family gathered around half past two in the afternoon to have lunch. Everyone felt like swimming after Rambod described his walk along the lake's promenade. Mandana wanted to speak to Jima without Sima catching wind of it, but it was difficult as the two sisters were sat by each other. Sima was smiling radiantly and talking to Karl. Her apparent joy was not due to conversing with Karl, but mainly to the thought of the guest she was expecting but whom she had yet to announce to everybody. Karl too seemed pleased - he was grinning from ear to ear, remembering the intense hour he had spent hidden in the garden with Mandana. Even the prospect that he may have made Mandana pregnant did not bother him.

Mandana, on the other hand, however, was regretful. She no longer wished for Karl to touch her. She could not wait to leave *Ganjbaran*, but before then she wanted to pay one last visit to what she regarded as the 'providential' pit. She got up and discretely asked Jima to follow her. She was expecting Sima to get all worked up about her behaviour and quiz her about what she had just whispered into Jima's ear, but to her surprise Sima continued smiling and told them both:

"*Go and enjoy the sun of Kashmir. One has to enjoy every single moment as one doesn't know what could happen next.*"

This, Mandana felt, was a pointed remark, which made her suspicious of Sima.

Once Mandana and Jima left the room, Mandana said:

"*I think Sima is up to something. Do you think she has been in our rooms and through our bags?*"

"*Let's go via our rooms – that's one way of finding out,*" replied Jima.

Both women came out of their rooms with empty bags, and confirmed to each other that all their bags and clothes were intact and that nothing appeared to have been touched.

"*As Sima put it, let's go and enjoy the sun of Kashmir in our own way and gather some more jewels,*" suggested Mandana.

"*I thought you were against the idea of collecting more gems,*" reminded her Jima.

"*Yes, it's true, but I am afraid we might regret letting this opportunity slip away,*" replied Mandana.

"*Let's leave it to the gods. If they are happy for us to take more, then we should.*"

On their way to the pit, Mandana complained to Jima about her slow pace. Jima retorted that she was no humming-bird and could not walk any faster, and that she shouldn't be so stressed out. But soon enough both women became quite distressed as they struggled to find the pit. They were convinced that they were in the right place, yet the ancient rectangular stone which had led them to the pit in the first place was nowhere to be seen. They must have spent at least three hours unsuccessfully trying to locate it. Exhausted, surely, but mostly frustrated, they headed back to the palace. Jima then turned to her niece and said:

"My beautiful girl, always remember this: opportunity only knocks once. I am glad that we had taken enough gems and jewellery when we had a chance to do so. But perhaps the gods believe that we had taken enough and hence they hid the rest of the treasure from us in order to leave some for future generations."

Mandana was too confused and tired to bother responding to this. Both women walked towards the palace, Jima persistently talking and Mandana persistently not listening. By the time they reached the palace, it was nearly seven-o-clock. Everybody had gathered in the main reception. Mandana could hear a man's voice that, though was familiar, was, neither Bahram's nor Karl's. *'Could it be that another member of the family has decided to visit them in India?'* she thought to herself. She entered the reception hall and got the shock of her life. Sebastian was involved in an in-depth conversation with Sima about monuments. As soon as Sebastian saw Mandana, he sprang towards her, hugged and kissed her under the steely gaze of Karl, who believed that no other man had the right to touch his newly acquired mistress. Mandana, on the other hand, didn't devote much thought to her affair with Karl. She was very anxious to know what had been discussed between Sima and Sebastian.

Sebastian retreated a step while tenderly holding Mandana's hands and said:

"I see you are not wearing the brooch I gave you! Have you already tired of it?"

Jima then appeared behind Mandana and although she too was stunned to see Sebastian, she did not bat an eyelid. She greeted him in an overly affected way and sat down next to Sima. Chetra then came and announced that dinner was about to be served, and led the family to the formal dining room. Both Sebastian and Karl wanted to sit by Mandana. Mandana, who generally enjoyed men's company and flirted tirelessly with them, was silent. Her failure to find the pit of gems that day had discouraged her. Sebastian's arrival had distressed her further. Her recent affair with a married man, a man who was married to her cousin, exasperated her even more. The last thing she wanted was to be sitting beside a male entity.

Mona, on the other hand, suspected nothing. She was very content to be surrounded by her husband, children and extended family. Since Mandana was not flirting with Karl, Mona was not worried. Karl on the other hand was quite frustrated. He could not understand what was going on in Mandana's head.

No woman - neither Western nor Eastern - had ever rejected him. However, Mandana was of a hybrid culture of her own. She could have a sexually liberated and detached attitude as what some might associate with North European or North American women, but, in reality, she aspired to be the virtuous woman that her own culture dictated. Such a schizophrenic approach to her romantic or sexual endeavours with members of the opposite sex confused many people – be they family or friends. Men on the other hand interpreted this oscillation as reflective of her desire to be elusive and mysterious, in the vain hope that she maintain her allure over them. Those who were planning to conquer her enjoyed the game; those who had already been involved with her resented it but could not resist her.

Delighted to see that the white table cloth hid half of his body from people's field of vision, Karl put his hands on Mandana's leg. Mandana brushed his hand off forcefully. Karl's face turned red, he was furious.

Mona did not even notice that Karl was upset, as she had never seen him be in such state. She thought that he had eaten something spicy, and advised him to have some mandarin juice and then pass her the jug. Azar on the other hand was observing Karl, Mandana and Sebastian carefully, and sensed some tension. She started her questions:

"*So Sebastian, have you come all the way to Kashmir to kidnap one of our girls?*"

"*Why would it be necessary to resort to kidnapping, when there is mutual attraction?*" replied Sebastian.

"*All this sounds quite serious,*" said Bahram. "*A young man coming all the way from the capital to a distant palace in Kashmir to see a girl surely must have honourable intentions.*"

"*I don't need to hide the facts, as both Ms Jima and Mandana know,*" said Sebastian. "*I have already asked Mandana to marry me, and I have come here to get her answer.*"

"*A man who offers a woman such a beautiful brooch,*" remarked Sima with a smile, "*must surely be really in love. So, Mandana, are we going to have a wedding soon?*"

For a minute Mandana was tempted to accept Sebastian's proposition, but the word brooch struck her mind suddenly. She remembered that there were a number of factors that she needed to take into consideration.

While Mandana was being questioned, Karl was fuming. He got up and spilt a glass of mandarin juice on Mandana's dress without anybody realising that it was done intentionally.

"*I am so sorry Mandana,*" said Karl. "*Let me take you to the kitchen and I will help you wipe the stains.*"

Jima interrupted:

"*There is no need for that, my dear son,*" and then she turned to Mandana. "*Let's go upstairs. You change, and give me the soiled dress and I will remove the stain.*"

Karl could hardly keep his composure and had to restrain himself from arguing with Jima. He knew he could not win against Jima. In order to dissimulate his frustration, he got up to fetch himself some liquor:

"*Would anyone like some banana liquor?*"

Poor Options

O nce in the room, Jima said in a motherly tone:
"*My beautiful daughter, I am worried for you. You looked so subdued at the table. It seemed as if you were being pushed into something for which you were not prepared. If Sima were a decent aunt, she would have first of all warned us about this worthless man's visit and never mentioned the word wedding in front of him. The woman really doesn't care about her family. I think that time has come for us to leave. This place has become too unhealthy. Sima is determined to wring our secret out of us, and with the help of Azar she might get us into trouble. As for my daughter's promiscuous husband, he seems to have developed a particular interest in you. I am afraid that you will soon be one of his victims and give in to his advances.*"

Mandana was indeed perplexed. She remained silent. She was unusually compliant and acquiescing towards her aunt – quite unlike her usual vivacious and defiant self. She was overwhelmed by a sense of powerlessness – the events that were unfolding around her, she felt, could not be contained by her and were not sympathetic to her needs and desires. She felt that she was losing control over her future and others were making decisions for her. This was one of those moments she felt totally incapable of applying her reason and her maturity to questions that seemed too complex – she was facing a dilemma and was paralysed by indecisiveness. She did not know what the right decision was: should she marry Sebastian, or leave with her aunt for an unknown destination?

She suddenly looked at her aunt with eyes wide open. In this state of indecisiveness, she felt this profound impulse to break free. She turned to the door and dashed, like a gazelle, out of the room, wearing still her stained dress. She avoided the main hall in order not to be seen by the rest of the people, and slid from the doors of the drawing room into the garden. She took a deep breath, and meditated for a few minutes. Once her mind was cleared, she decided to consider Sebastian's marriage proposal first: she was neither in love with him, nor willing to settle for a man she did not think could fulfil her dreams. Her second option was to leave with Jima. But was there really any point to this? Jima was a burden and a very difficult person to bear. None of these two options to her provided any meaningful solution.

A New Departure

Indeed, Mandana longed to get married but not at any cost for the sake of it. She wanted to fall in love and experience all the anguish and passion that this engendered. She was thinking of what Sima had advised her when she had first arrived in India. She had not pursued her studies, and she believed that many men might perceive this as a flaw. Mandana did not enjoy studying, but thought she needed to compensate for her lack of interest in books by acquiring a special skill. Fashion and cosmetics had always been a passion, and therefore she thought she might enrol on a fashion design course. She made up her mind. She was going to leave within the next 48 hours. She knew that it would be near impossible for Jima to follow her, given how with her Iranian passport it was likely she would face many travel restrictions and would need visas for most places to which Mandana would want to travel. Considering her plans to enrol on a fashion design course, Mandana thought it best to first visit New York and experience all the excitements that the Big Apple had to offer her.

Suddenly, she was thrilled to have made this decision. She felt that once again she was in charge of her own destiny. She ran upstairs to her room and changed. Jima had gone back to join the rest of the family, leaving Mandana behind. Mandana did not deal with the stain. She just took off her dress and put on a beautiful turquoise sari adorned with golden embroidered patterns. She returned downstairs conscious of the likelihood that her dress would scandalise both Karl and Sebastien. She wanted to enjoy being an enchantress despite the fact that neither man no longer interested her.

The following day, despite having gone to bed late, Mandana woke up earlier than the other residents of the palace. She called Maxime and announced that she was going to Delhi soon. While she was on the phone, Jima had woken up and come downstairs. She overheard Mandana's conversation and was quite upset. She decided to confront Mandana:

"My dear girl, you are now beginning to worry me. Last night you were flirting relentlessly with two men at the dining table, and, from what I heard, tomorrow you are planning to meet another one for a romantic journey who knows where. Have you decided to leave with Maxime for Europe surreptitiously?"

Mandana was conscious that how she had behaved recently was ripe for being misunderstood and provided ample fodder to anyone who would want to speculate on her motives, and said:

"I wasn't planning to leave secretly this time, but time has come for me to move on. As you, yourself, mentioned we shouldn't stay here longer."

"That is right my daughter," acknowledged Jima. *"However, remember that the world is a jungle, and a young, beautiful, wealthy woman is good prey for cunning and ruthless men. I am not advising that you necessarily live with a relative, but I seriously advise you to consider living somewhere you have other members of your family nearby. They will give you moral support when you need it, and will protect you. Going off by yourself isn't the most sensible decision you have ever made."*

"My goal isn't to run away from my family," assured Mandana her aunt. *"I am too old for that. I want to stay in touch with my relatives and visit them, including you regularly. I also don't believe in making my own mistakes; life is too short and one needs to learn from other people's experiences. I will definitely turn to my family for advice whenever I feel this is necessary. But I want to take advantage of my youth and financial independence. I don't want my life to be controlled by my father or an aunt. We can't stay here eternally anyway. As you said yourself, Sima is a very difficult person to live with and once the rest of the family has left, she is going to give us a hard time. I want to leave while I can still keep good memories of Ganjbaran, and I recommend that you do the same, and start planning your departure now. Since you need visas for practically everywhere, perhaps you should visit one of these embassies in New Delhi soon."*

Jima realised that Mandana was too clever to be conned into living with her. However, she did not want to stay behind in *Ganjbaran* with Sima alone. She thought quickly of a solution and said:

"*Since Mona lives in London, I should move there. We have a few cousins scattered all over the city as well. Maybe you should move to London too. It's an exciting place with lots of opportunities and entertainment for young people.*"

"*I am planning to move to New York for a couple of years to study design,*" asserted Mandana.

"*My beautiful daughter, you might carry a European passport but if you are travelling to America, you will also need a visa. Perhaps we could travel together to Delhi and apply for visas.*"

"*The queues are endless at the American embassy in Delhi; I would be better off going to Europe and getting my visa there,*" said Mandana.

"*In all cases, you can't possibly send your old aunt alone to Delhi,*" insisted Jima. "*You should come all the way to London with me, get your visa sorted out in London and then move to New York. You have to also promise me that you will spend most of your holidays with your relatives in London.*"

"*We will see,*" replied Mandana. "*For the time being let's plan our journey to New Delhi! Maxime is going to be delighted to see you return with me.*"

"*I bet,*" concluded Jima with a tinge of sarcasm, and produced her peculiar hen-like noise to convey her delight.

THE MISSED HAPPINESS

Mandana and Jima went upstairs to pack once again. The older woman needed help with the packing.

Whilst folding clothes, Mandana said:

"*Once in New York, I am sure I will be very happy.*"

"*Happiness isn't something you have to run after,*" said Jima, "*it's always with you. With its picturesque gardens and its purple marbles, this palace looks like paradise. In addition, both of us know that it has many hidden treasures. We were all impressed with it and yet now we all want to leave. If we learn to appreciate what we have, and enjoy every moment that life has given us, then we can be happy anywhere and everywhere. Sima, I believe has been a bad influence here. She has everything to be happy, and yet she isn't, otherwise why would we have wanted to leave Ganjbaran?*"

"*What is the source of Sima's grudge against the world?*" asked Mandana.

"*Failing at university,*" replied Jima.

"*The way she reprimanded me for havi ng left university, I thought she had many degrees,*" said Mandana surprised.

"*Precisely. Sima is obsessed with diplomas, because she doesn't have any herself. Just mention the word university in front her, and you will see what will happen. She will tell you a bunch of lies, and if you challenge her, and remind her that she has no degrees, she will get violent, to the point that she will break anything she finds within her reach.*"

"*Really? Surely, she must be insane. She did not study for the sake of money and now she envies penniless academics.*"

"*Some people no matter what the gods give them, are unsatisfied. They will always have hang-ups, and envy even people who have miserable lives.*"

"If she did not study, what did she do then?"

"My sister did get a worthless diploma from a worthless college in a small American town, which hardly counts as a Bachelor's. But even for that it took her seven or eight years. She was too busy chasing men, trying to catch a handsome rich heir."

"And that did not work out?"

"No. And there were torrents of tears. She was dumped many a time that I believe she lost faith in men and dedicated herself to a career. One of the young men with whom she had an affair pitied her and asked his father to give her a job in his soap factory. From that point, destiny took another turn for her and she became a successful woman."

Intrigued by Jima's source of information, Mandana asked:

"How do you know all these stories? I doubt that Sima would have told them to you herself."

"It's a small world. Her flatmate in the US happened to be the daughter of one of my neighbours in Tehran. Since Sima is very good in alienating her friends, the young woman developed a strong dislike for her. Once she returned to Tehran we met by accident at a neighbour's dinner party. As soon as she found out that I was Sima's sister, she told a few neighbours everything she knew about Sima. Until then my neighbours envied me, as they couldn't find anything to disrepute me. With gossip about Sima in hand, some stupid neighbours thought that they could hurt me by discussing Sima's private life in every nook and cranny. They were quite disappointed when they saw that I continued to keep my head up and ignored them. A couple of years later, the Revolution took place and Sima's anecdotes were forgotten, at least by the neighbours. Obviously, Sima was quite distressed when she found out that I knew all about her adventures in America. She wanted to strangle her ex-flatmate, but the latter had suddenly vanished amidst the Revolution."

"If I had the patience to write a book, I would definitely entitle it: 'Sima and her Invisible Diploma,'" giggled Mandana, while Jima cackled in her corner.

Two Slaps and a Shake

M andana was enjoying Jima's gossiping, but her smile vanished when she realised that she was not the only one. Azar had managed to come downstairs unnoticed, and had heard everything Jima had said about Sima. When Azar realised that Mandana had noticed her, she tried to pretend that she was on her way to the kitchen. Mandana called Azar's name out loud and bade her good morning. Azar went towards the two women greeting them warmly and complimenting them for being such early risers. Jima did not bother answering Azar back. She turned to her and Mandana and said:

"I wonder who else is up and eavesdropping."

As Azar opened her mouth to say something, Jima interrupted her and continued:

"I am extremely hungry now. I need to eat something right away. Let's go to the kitchen, ladies."

On their way they met Mona and her children who were also looking forward to breakfast. Not long after, the husbands, Sebastian and Azar's children joined them. Only Sima was missing.

Once at the breakfast table, Bahram inquired about Sima's whereabouts and said that he missed her. Azar took over the conversation saying that she missed her too, and praised her for her generosity:

"I am so grateful to her for having taken care of my family's travel expenses all the way from Canada to India. She is such a dear soul for bringing us all here to share this piece of paradise. We don't have two of her kind in our family."

"My dear Azar," began Jima. *"You clearly don't know my sister very well. Since her childhood, Sima never gave anything to anyone for free. When she was a little girl, she would only lend you ribbons, flowers and handkerchiefs, and as soon*

106

as you contradicted her, she would take them back from you. She would never, ever give you sweets or chocolates as she knew she couldn't reclaim them. My daughter, believe me, Sima is expecting something from you in return. I would watch out if I were you."

"*Mother,*" intervened Mona, "*don't you think that you are being too harsh on your sister? After all, she has offered you hospitality when you couldn't afford to buy a home abroad and none of your other siblings wanted to see you.*"

Mona's words hurt Jima deeply as she felt humiliated and belittled in front of the rest of the family, especially that those words were uttered by her own daughter. She always wanted to project a good image of herself, but her daughter had now conveyed to everyone that she was resented and badly off.

Jima turned to her daughter and said:

"*My little daughter, how could you make such an idiotic statement? Didn't you realise that I had felt sorry for my younger sister for being all by herself in exile? I could have perfectly well gone elsewhere. You can't possibly be aware of my reasons and my financial situation. I did not need Sima to pay for my airfare like Azar and her family. As you know, just by pawning my emerald brooch I could rent an entire plane and travel around the world.*"

"*But mother, you did not have that brooch when you left Iran, you told us yesterday how you received it ....*"

Jima did not let Mona finish her sentence. She got up and slapped her daughter as hard as she could across the face, and left the room, bumping into Sima who was eavesdropping behind the door. Jima said as loud as possible so that everyone could hear:

"*Apparently eavesdropping has become the fashion in this place!*" and with a slightly lower voice she told Sima, "*Don't you have anything better to do?*"

Sima, who had heard all of Jima's comments in the breakfast room, yearned also to slap her sister in the face; however, the family code dictated that a younger sister could not afford to give herself such a pleasure. She just pulled Jima forcefully towards her and said:

"*How dare you say such horrible things behind my back?*"

Jima, capitalising on society's strictures that the younger ought to respect the senior, retorted:

"*Watch your manners.*"

"*I take no lectures on manners from you,*" thundered Sima angrily. "*I am unable to put up with your appalling attitude any longer.*"

"*You won't have to,*" replied Jima in a baleful tone. "*As soon as I have my ticket sorted out, I will leave and I don't want to see your face ever again.*"

Hearing this, Sima could not contain her outrage and slapped Jima across her face. Jima who had anticipated the scene, was fully prepared to return her sister's aggression. She returned Sima's slap as hard as she could. Sima nearly fell on the floor. Nobody expected a woman of Jima's age to have such powerful hands.

As Sima was recovering from the slap and looking with bewildered eyes at Jima, Jima screamed as loud as she could in order to avoid Sima's retaliation. Everyone suddenly left Mona to see what was happening. Mona, who yearned for attention when she cried, ended up sobbing alone.

Seeing that she could not attack Jima in full view of all her guests, Sima ran upstairs to Jima's room and began throwing her clothes down the stairs. At this point, Mandana started to panic as she was afraid that Sima might find another piece of jewellery, she ran upstairs, instinctively gripped Sima forcefully by her upper arms and shook her for a few moments. Sima became hysterical and started shouting at Mandana, telling her to leave her palace on the spot. Sima was also about to slap her in the face, but Mandana intercepted her hand, and avered in a calm yet forceful voice:

"*For the sake of your reputation before your own family, try to control yourself! Bear us one more day. We are leaving tomorrow on the first available plane. You couldn't possibly throw two women out in the wilderness like this in front of Azar. Surely you can foresee how she will report the incident to the whole world, and you will never be able to face any member of the family again.*"

Sima was overwhelmed by the situation. She had been verbally and physically abused without any apparent support or solidarity from her family, who surely must have shared her outrage at Jima's transgressions. She had been bad-mouthed, slapped in the face, and physically shaken. And to add insult to injury, she was now being denied the right to seek to assert herself in what, after all, was her property. She could not take it any longer. Tears streamed down her face.

Mandana was overwhelmed by sympathy for her aunt. She weakened her rigid grip and gently pulled her towards her and gave her a heartfelt strong hug. She then said she was sorry that her aunt had had to put up with so much in the past few days and to have been treated with such ingratitude.

"*Let's go to the kitchen and prepare a feast for our last day at the palace,*" suggested Mandana.

Sima, now softened, turned to Mandana and asked:

"*Where do you plan to go? I don't think you should take Jima with you. You will end up becoming hysterical like me. You would be better off alone with Sebastian.*"

"*I am not planning to travel with either of them,*" explained Mandana. "*However, Jima is afraid to travel by herself to New Delhi to sort out the visa situation, and hopes to accompany me until she reaches her final destination.*"

"*Mandana, I think Jima is trying hard to fool you. She neither has the moral strength nor the financial ability to live all by herself. Unless some miracle has happened and she has discovered a mine of diamonds nearby, you had better keep away from her.*"

Mandana did not wish to continue the conversation, as she felt that Sima was trying to gather information from her. Therefore, as soon as they reached the kitchen she called Chetra and asked her to help them prepare a pomegranate stew, along with a quince *Khoresh*. Azar joined them in the kitchen and decided to prepare a *Javaher polo* along with the fruity stews.

GANJBARAN, THE PALACE OF FIGHT AND TEARS

In the evening, the table was filled with all sorts of sweet Persian winter dishes, most of which had been prepared by Azar. The scent of rice and saffron had drawn everybody to the dining room. Jima was the last one to come. She sat next to Bahram, and he opened the conversation with her. It was actually the first time ever Bahram and Jima were directly conversing. Bahram talked about the trips he had actually made and Jima about journeys she had never taken. She was a master of inventing stories on the spot, and recounted them with such an intensity that anyone lacking prior knowledge of Jima and her delusions would surely believe her. One of her travel stories was a direct telling of a story contained in the collection of the *Thousand and One Nights*. Sima and Mona were simultaneously talking to Karl who chose to respond first to Sima. Mona felt that her husband should have given her the priority. She was so furious to be neglected that she could not control herself. Instead of scolding her husband, she poured her anger on Sima, as she was scared that her husband would find a pretext to hurt her in some other way:

"Why do you always think you have the priority over others? Where are your manners?"

Sima wanted to retaliate but Azar interrupted by offering her some *naan*. Sima suddenly burst into tears.

"I have always striven to gather the family together and see to their well-being, and all I get in return is hostility and cruel words. If all of you hate me so much, why are you here visiting me in my palace?"

Mona began wailing, got off her chair and left the room. Karl reluctantly went to console his wife. Azar remained beside Sima and took her into her arms, trying to appease her. Jima turned to Mandana and said:

"Take advantage of this moment. While Sima is crying, go and call the airport and see to our departure."

Sebastian who was sitting beside Mandana, turned and said:

"You shouldn't worry about your plane, ladies. Just tell me your destination and I will take care of everything."

Mandana did not know what to do. She could not possibly land in New Delhi with Jima and Sebastian. Their sight would irritate Maxime to such an extent that he might refuse to assist her with her journey. Now that Jima wanted to follow her to Europe, she definitely needed Maxime's help to secure Jima a visa and a seat on a plane, as her aunt did not even have a ticket. Since Sebastian had become a burden, she had to find a way to rid herself of him. Mandana did not say anything to Sebastian, and left the room to make her call. Sebastian followed her. Karl came back from another entrance to fetch Mona's purse and saw his rival pursuing Mandana. He left the purse and went after them. Once at the phone, Mandana turned to both men and snapped:

"Would you mind not following me around like pets? Sebastian, I think it's time for you to leave. I have given your marriage proposal some thought, and I have come to realise that I don't want to get married at this point. I plan to continue my studies now, and wish to be single for another three years at least."

"Allow me then to spend another few days with you," pleaded Sebastian. *"We can't possibly part like this."*

"You heard the young lady," intervened Karl. *"She wants you to leave."*

"Who are you to meddle yourself in our business?" snarled Sebastian.

As Sebastian finished his sentence, Karl with his fist struck him in the face. A fight between them ensued. Hearing the fight, Bahram and his sons dashed to separate the men.

Meanwhile, Mandana took the phone, pulled its long cord as far as possible from the crowd and called Maxime. She depicted herself as a caring niece who could not possibly leave her old aunt behind and needed him to arrange her trip from *Ganjbaran* to New Delhi, and thereafter to London. She added:

"And bear in mind that my aunt has an Iranian passport and needs a visa to travel to England."

Maxime promised to assist her. He also hinted that he wished to spend an entire night in Mandana's company without Jima. Mandana led him on. Meanwhile she was to wait for Maxime's confirmation.

Bahram was trying to reconcile Karl and Sebastian. Both men stopped listening to him when Mandana reappeared in front of them. Mandana had finished her phone call and was on her way to the veranda. She did not even look at the men. From the veranda, she saw Jima, Azar and Sima gathered around a big black cauldron in the garden making saffron pudding. They had adopted the old-fashioned style of making this delicacy by laying the cauldron on rocks, with a wood fire lit underneath. Jima's saffron pudding was very popular with the family, and Azar and Sima wanted to learn her secret.

Mandana was pleasantly surprised to see Sima all serene without any traces of tears. Sima was not the type of person to indulge her feelings for too long.

When Mandana joined them, Azar was talking about her dream to leave Canada and move to London or New York. She said that she found life in Vancouver uninspiring and that she felt somewhat at the edge of the world. She ended her complaint by saying that she was in no position to make any decisions as all depended on her husband finding a job in another city. Disinterested in Azar's dreams, Jima conducted her own speech about London, saying that it was a wonderful city and that before the Iranian Revolution she used to travel there at least twice a year to visit Mona:

"*Mona took me every day to Holland Park where I spent my time watching the peacocks, geese and many colourful exotic birds whose names I couldn't remember. For some reasons they all seemed to connect with me as if I were one of them. I wouldn't mind living there for a couple of years.*"

Perhaps because of her reference to birds, Jima's voice reminded them all, more than ever, of a rooster's croak. Azar and Mandana burst into laughter and in order to avoid explanations, Azar quickly picked a grim subject:

"*This Revolution has been a serious blow to all of us. We have become so disoriented that we are not able to decide where we want to live. It's so difficult to settle and anchor our lives somewhere and call it home. I wonder how my sons regard Vancouver. My eldest, Pedram, listens to Persian music, and most of his friends are*

Iranian as well. But at the same time, despite the nostalgia he has for his country, he seems to be quite happy."

"*I wouldn't worry too much about your sons,*" said Sima. "*They seem to have adapted well to life in Canada. And anyway, North America is a promised land for youngsters. There are so many opportunities there for them. They can fulfil their dreams if only they set their mind to a profession. Things would have been probably different if they were living in continental Europe where generally doors are closed to immigrants.*"

Mandana was impatient to try the saffron pudding despite its not being ready. Jima prevented her from dipping a spoon into the cauldron and squawked:

"*Don't you dare touch the pudding before I have added the almonds! Go in the kitchen and see if you can find some sweets there.*"

Mandana went in the kitchen and opened the refrigerator. She saw a big box of green tangerines. She peeled one and could not believe how sweet it was. She had never had such a tasty tangerine in her life, '*What kind of a soil yields fruit with such a unique flavour?*' thought Mandana to herself; '*India is such a magical land.*' As she was about to take another one, the phone rang. She dashed out of the kitchen as she thought it was Maxime.

The phone call was from her eldest aunt Atoossa. Sima came in the hall and took the phone from Mandana. She asked Atoossa where she was. Atoossa recounted her woes with her visa dilemmas, and how she had ended up in Spain as it was one of the rare countries she could enter without one. Her daughter was in Italy living in her old villa in the outskirts of Rome, and she was hoping to get a visa in the coming days. Sima invited her to Kashmir, but Atoossa said that she was too old for such a long journey.

While Sima was talking to Atoossa, Jima managed to pour the saffron pudding into a big serving dish and decorate it with cinnamon and pistachios. As soon as Mandana told her that Sima was on the phone with Atoossa, she hurried to the phone before Sima could hang up. Jima asked Atoossa the same questions as Sima, and then instead of inviting her to Sima's place - a transgression she so often practiced - she invited herself to Italy:

"*My adorable sister, we should both settle in Rome. Italians are so similar to Iranians, I am sure we are not going to get homesick there. I have decided to purchase a flat in the historical centre of Rome not far from the Colosseum. You should come and live with me in order not to burden your daughter.*"

Atoossa was taking Jima's offer with a hefty pinch of salt as she knew about her sister's chronic impecuniousness. She regarded this as Jima's custom of aggrandising her social position and wealth – it was a game of charades that the family partook of in almost a schizophrenic manner: on the one hand, conscious of the delusions of Jima and of the lack of substance of her claims, and on the other, their acquiescing to indulge Jima in pretending that they found her flights of fancy convincing.

Worthless Degrees

While Jima was on the phone, Sima ushered Azar to one of the bedrooms upstairs where she had stored all the handicrafts and artefacts she had purchased at the markets in Delhi, Simla and Srinagar. Besides decorative items and shawls, Sima had bought a number of old manuscripts dating back to the Mughal era. She wanted to prove to Azar that she was a scholar, and that she was ahead of the rest of her family both intellectually and financially. Azar was herself a housewife with barely a high school diploma, with no real interest in scholarly works. However, Sima continued boasting about her academic achievements and delivered a lengthy lecture on her Master's degree that prompted Azar to ask her field of studies. Jima had finished her conversation with Atoossa and was eavesdropping at their conversation. She was offended by Sima's need to undermine the entire family in order to flatter herself. As soon as Azar inquired about Sima's Master's degree topic, Jima entered and answered in Sima's stead:

"She has an MA in urinology."

Although Azar had nothing against Sima that would cause her to use this as an opportunity to ridicule her, she could not help but find Jima's sarcastic remark supremely amusing.

Education was Sima's weakness, and Jima, quite deliberately, had struck a soft spot. Jima's comment made Sima hysterical once again. She unrolled all the saris and dropped them on the floor. She came up with the most insulting words she could devise. Azar tried to calm Sima down, telling her that having a Master's degree was not all that mattered, and that being a kind person was what really counted. Jima was so satisfied to see Sima in that state that she did not want to leave the room.

"*I have done everything in my power to help this monster of a sister,*" said Sima. "*But she is so jealous of me that she couldn't help hissing her venom whenever she can. She hasn't a penny to her name and has barely an eighth-grade certificate and yet here she is commenting about my educational endeavours.*"

Jima got very upset by hearing these words, as she too had recounted whenever she had the opportunity that before getting married she had started studying towards a doctoral degree in Germany when by misfortune she had been made to marry her husband and had therefore been forced to renounce her studies. However, Jima maintained her composure and retorted right away:

"*I would rather stick to an eighth-grade certificate than be humiliated for eight years striving to get a Bachelor's degree from a rubbish community college in Kentucky. My dear sister, your education is worth less than a gramme of manure.*"

Sima could have strangled Jima. Mandana entered the room at the right time to prevent a further family tragedy. She took Jima's arm and pulled her out of the room. Jima however could not stop denigrating Sima. Sima and Azar could still hear her comments while she was being hauled away:

"*I don't understand why Sima persists in displaying herself as a scholar when she could hardly sit down and read five lines. She used to spot good students and ask them to summarise books for her verbally so that she could go and involve herself in intellectual discussions. She would attend gatherings during which she would comment about books and articles she had never seen in her life. Her only purpose was to impress wealthy young men whose usual hangouts were these scholarly circles.*"

By this time, they had reached Jima's room and Mandana had closed the door behind her. Jima continued her speech, unaffected by the new decor:

"*Sima would then target one of the young men who had had the misfortune of having spoken to her, and she would then open her web as wide as possible in order to trap the poor man into marriage. Well, we all know the outcome of that strategy already – she has remained on the shelf.*"

"*What is your point of repeating Sima's personal history to everyone?*" asked Mandana. "*As you said, I have already heard these stories before. Attacking your sister like that, and ruining her reputation in front of Azar, can only be damaging to yourself. If I were you I would only focus on my own travel dilemma. You need to pack as we are leaving soon. If I were Sima, I wouldn't want to see your face a day longer.*"

"*On whose side are you?*" asked Jima.

The telephone rang. Mandana did not bother answering Jima, and dashed out to answer the call.

Azar did not leave Sima, despite the fact that Sima had belittled her earlier by insinuating that she was uneducated. Azar felt that her relative needed consolation, therefore she hugged Sima and said:

"*Don't let yourself be affected by other people's comments. You have had a successful life up to now. Education is important, but not to the extent of getting angry over people's comments regarding your diplomas. People attend university, wear themselves out, to get a profession that would allow them to make a living. You have done far better than 99% of the world. You have a beautiful palace in India that any monarch would envy.*"

Unfortunately, Sima was not comforted by Azar's words. Like most human beings she was not satisfied with what she had, and was obsessed by university diplomas that she did not. She knew that Azar with all her kindness was extremely keen on gossip and was certainly going to broadcast the hot news to the rest of the family. Sima dreaded becoming the laughing stock of the Gilipours.

Sima wiped her tears once again, pushed her hair back and said:

"*You know Azar, it isn't what Jima said about my degrees that hurt me, it's all this animosity that she expresses against me that saddens me. She has been mean to me since the loss of her daughter, and since she has grown older, her attitude towards me has only deteriorated. I have always tried to be gentle with her, and take care of her despite all the nasty things that she has said about me. As you can see, I have offered her my home, and look how she repays me. Knowing that she had not finished school and would be jealous if I mentioned that I had obtained my Master's, I did not tell her anything about my academic achievements after returning from the United States.*"

Azar was beginning to feel sorry for Sima until she reverted back to the topic on her non-existent degrees. Thus, for what seemed like hours, Sima exasperated Azar with her imaginary academic qualifications, until Azar said she desperately needed a cup of tea or else she would get a headache. She got up and left the room saturated by all the drama, but had already decided that she preferred Jima's version. She went down the stairs with glee about banking one more juicy story for all the absent relatives.

Some Time to Ponder

Sima was left alone in the room with her own thoughts. Even if Azar had believed her lies, she could not convince herself that she possessed a Master's degree. And sadly for her, Jima had highlighted the truth. It had indeed taken her eight years to obtain a Bachelor's degree, and even that was a lucky break: she had hardly concentrated on her studies. Now, she regretted having wasted so much of her time in the US chasing after men. Kentucky was a boring place to be, but at that time she had neither the financial means nor outstanding marks to attend an Ivy League college. This however had not prevented her from travelling to New England and spending most of her time on the campuses of Harvard and Yale, seducing young Iranian men. Instead of attending lectures in Kentucky, she had made marriage her priority, and had ended sleeping with many handsome and rich students without securing an engagement ring.

Sima wished to blame her family's education pretences and aspirations for her promiscuity during her youth and for failing at university, but neither of her sisters had had pre or extra-marital affairs. Her eldest sister, Atoossa, was an accomplished woman for her generation. She had studied hydrology at the University of Rome, and was hired immediately upon graduation by Luxembourg's water company. After five years in Luxembourg she decided to return to Tehran in 1953 despite the political havoc created by the CIA after the conspired removal of the nationalist Prime Minister, Mossadegh. During that time, Iran suffered from a shortage of highly skilled people, and Atoossa was offered an executive position on a silver tray: she was nominated the head of Tehran's water company.

By then, unmarried Atoossa was considered past her prime and the only suitors she got were a few middle-aged widowed wealthy men. Despite the fact that she had not even reached thirty, she gave in to family pressure and married one of them.

Sima thought she could not possibly have envied her sister who married a man twenty-six years her senior and who left her widowed with one child after just three years of marriage. And her other sister, Jima, despite the fact that she got married at the age of twenty-four to a man who loved her, was one of the unhappiest women she knew. Jima did not like her husband, and made his life miserable after the loss of her first daughter. She never demonstrated any affection towards her second daughter, let alone anyone else. Sima struggled to think of anyone that was fond of Jima.

Sima realised that her cousin, Azar, was right to a certain extent, and perhaps she should count her blessings from time to time. All the hysteria and deep thinking had made her hungry. She decided to go downstairs and call everybody to join her for dinner. She also cheered herself by thinking of Jima's immediate departure.

An Eventful Night

That night everyone was restless. Sebastian refused to leave without Mandana and was begging her to sleep with him. After dinner Mandana locked herself in her room as she wanted to pack without being disturbed. Sebastian knocked on two occasions on her door, but she refused to unlock and let him in. Seeing that Mandana refused to unlock the door for Sebastian, Karl decided to find another way to enter Mandana's room. At midnight Karl jumped into her room from the window, which was left ajar. Mandana did not bother screaming. She went towards Karl, slapped him hard in the face, and asked him to leave at once. Instead, he grabbed her and kissed her as passionately as he could. Mandana was too tired to sleep with anyone. She had already sampled what it was to be with Karl, and was left with no unsatisfied curiosity. She was tempted to kick him between the legs and just throw him out, but refrained from doing so. Karl was heavily breathing in his excited state. He was desperate for a word from Mandana, but a knock at the door ended the momentum. Mandana answered as loud as she could:

"*Who is it?*"

"*It's me, Jima, please open the door, my dear.*"

Mandana smiled as broadly as she could to Karl. Karl asked Mandana where he could hide. She answered him to leave through the window. Karl sulked and pulled a sad face, but Mandana turned her face away from him and went towards the door. Karl went back to the window and jumped. As Mandana turned the key, she heard a loud howl of pain from the window. Jima entered the room and asked:

"*What was that? Was that a human or an animal?*"

"*I don't know,*" replied Mandana.

"Let's have a look from the window," proposed Jima.

The lights stemming from the lanterns attached to the palace's walls were too weak, and as a result it was difficult to distinguish between a man and a beast. But then Jima and Mandana saw two shadows in the garden whispering to each other. Mandana was intrigued as she was wondering who else besides Karl was in the garden.

"Perhaps these are heavenly beings sent by the gods to convey some message," said Jima in an excited tone.

Jima was generally slow partly owing to her age, but she leapt whenever she was provoked or excited as if invigorated by some invisible force. Under the illusion that the gods were waiting downstairs for her, she dashed to the garden, ran towards the shadows and bumped into one of them going in the opposite direction.

"I am here, oh Lord, to honour your words and listen to your guidance," said Jima.

The shadow stopped and replied:

"Karl has bruised his foot. He doesn't know if it's broken or not. I need to wake up my parents."

Jima recognised Rambod's voice. She felt humiliated to the bone. She slapped the boy in the face and shouted as loud as she could Azar's name. She then continued insulting the boy, with abstruse terms the latter could not possibly understand as they were no longer used by common people.

Mona recognised her mother's voice and ran out of her room, meeting Azar, Bahram, Sima and Sebastian in the corridor. They all rushed downstairs to see Rambod being verbally abused by Jima and Karl moaning from the pain. Mona ran towards her husband. Sima followed her at a slower pace. Bahram and Azar went towards Jima and Rambod to see what had happened between them.

"Mummy, this crazy woman slapped me in the face as I said that Karl needs help" said Rambod. *"What is wrong with her?"*

Bahram who was rather annoyed that his son had been physically attacked said:

"Ms. Jima, what is indeed wrong with you?"

"*Mr Bahram,*" replied Jima, "*how dare you speak to me in such a tone. You don't know how to bring up your sons. This one has posed as a god! Does he want to bring divine wrath upon us? This is blasphemy. How can my sister be so stupid as to invite such profane and crude people?*"

Sima felt that she had to go and defend Azar and her husband.

"*Jima,*" said Sima, "*I am very glad that you are leaving soon. I hope that you will never have the chance to poison people's lives like this again.*"

"*Me poisoning lives? Me?*"

Mandana had not budged from her window, remaining the only spectator of the drama. She was dying from laughter. Azar pulled her son aside and asked him what he was doing in the garden in the middle of the night. He responded that his brother had monopolised the bathroom near their bedrooms and he had an urgent need to relieve himself. He said he had no time to look for a toilet in the palace and therefore he dashed outside, and while he was passing water, he saw a man falling from a window.

Azar no longer cared about what her son was doing, but was now more curious to find out which window it was from which Karl had fallen.

"*Which window was it?*" asked Azar.

Rambod could not satisfy his mother's curiosity. Azar, annoyed, told him off. Azar then dashed towards Karl and Mona in order to hear Karl's version of the story. As Karl was sitting on the grass and Mona was caressing his leg, Azar knelt towards the couple and asked:

"*So what happened?*"

Karl looked up and saw Rambod lingering nearby. He therefore knew that he could not lie completely. He had told him earlier that he had fallen trying to catch a bird. Sebastian, who was within earshot, was convinced that Karl had fallen from Mandana's window. He wanted to give Karl a hard time by alluding to his falling from Mandana's room, but as his first employer had taught him to think quickly and speak slowly, Sebastian pondered a few seconds to see if he had anything to gain from such a Machiavellian scheme, and indeed he did not. By ruining Karl's relation with Mona, he might free the man from the bonds of marriage and allow him to court Mandana overtly. He therefore decided to remain silent, since by experience he had never regretted what he had not said. Sebastian turned around and went upstairs, knocking once again on Mandana's door. Since Mandana was looking out from the window she knew it was Sebastian. She just replied:

"*I am in my pyjamas and can't possibly open the door in this state.*"

Sebastian tried to imitate Jima's voice, sounding like an ostrich:

"*Even if it were your aunt Jima?*"

"*Nice try, Sebastian,*" answered Mandana, "*but my aunt is still downstairs arguing with Azar and Sima.*"

"*Please let me in,*" begged Sebastian. "*I really need to speak to you.*"

Mandana shunned Sebastian's request:

"*Wait till tomorrow morning, as I am really not in any mood to talk. I am off to bed now. Good night!*"

Rambod arrived upstairs and saw Sebastian behind Mandana's room, and said:

"*It's obvious, she doesn't love you.*"

Sebastian chased Rambod to his room, and went frustrated back to his room, determined to make himself loved.

Downstairs the inquisition continued - excepting Jima, who was disappointed that the youngster wasn't some divine being, - the three other women were dying to know how Karl had hurt his leg, and Karl was pretending that he was in too much pain to answer. He asked Bahram and Mona to help him upstairs. Sima and Azar remained downstairs hoping to solve the mystery together.

"*So how do you think Karl managed to injure himself?*" asked Azar.

"*It looks as if he fell while climbing the wall,*" replied Sima.

"*Why would he do such a childish thing? It would have made sense if Rambod was climbing walls, but Karl?*"

"*Let's see. Whose bedroom is on this side? Mona and Karl's; their children's; Jima's and ...*" Sima slowed the pace of her utterance "*...Mandana's.*"

"*Are you insinuating that Karl and Mandana are having an affair?*"

"*It all makes sense now,*" said Sima. "*Do you remember Karl's frustration when he saw Sebastian, and then they had a fight together? Karl isn't a faithful husband; we all know that. And Mandana is a seductive young woman.*"

"*Yes Sima,*" acknowledged Azar. "*But why on earth would he still climb the wall, instead of just walking into Mandana's room?*"

"*These are just details. They might have just had a romantic fight, so that Mandana threw him out of the window. Let's go to bed as it's quite late.*"

Careworn Mother, Careless Grandmother

Once again, the following morning no one was able to get up early except Mandana. She dashed downstairs to call Maxime. Jima had woken up slightly later and knocked at Mandana's room. Since she did not get any reply she went to the kitchen and found Mandana eating tangerines.

"*Are we finally leaving today?*"

"*Unfortunately, no. Maxime said that he is caught up with some airline business, but has booked our plane for tomorrow early in the afternoon. A car is going to come and pick us up tomorrow morning. He has also booked you an appointment with the British High Commissioner the day after tomorrow so that you can get your visa right away. Just bear Sima another day and it will soon be over.*"

At noon the sun was shining high above the palace, the flowers of the garden were responding to the sun's calling, and fluttering their leaves. Inside, in the living room, a golden lamp was still lit, but its light was hardly visible due to the ubiquity of the sun's flooding rays. An antique Indian water clock stirred a beautiful melody from the reception hall. Mona's children were awake and had breakfasted earlier with Mandana and Jima. Jima had sent them out to play in the garden. She had watched over them for about fifteen minutes and then left them to their own devices. Mandana, with whom she had wanted to catch up, had gone for a walk.

At noon Mona went to her children's room. As they were not there she looked for them downstairs and at the veranda. She was suddenly panic stricken. She dashed upstairs to wake up Karl. Karl forgot his pain in his foot. He quickly put a shirt and a pair of jeans on, and the couple ran downstairs calling out for their children and looking for them everywhere. Their voices woke the rest of the family up. Sima, Azar and her family, and Sebastian all came downstairs and went to the garden. Mona pleaded with them to help with finding their children. They had to leave the vicinity of the building immediately, and search in the fields and the bushes. Azar, Bahram and their sons grabbed some tangerines from the kitchen, distributed them among everybody. Mona refused to eat. Azar did not insist. She asked Pedram and Rambod to take different directions. And everyone split taking their own path, shouting, "*Som, Kouros.*"

An hour later, Jima and Mandana finished their stroll and returned to the palace. Chetra had just prepared some *dal* and rice. Mandana carped why their lunch was so frugal. Chetra explained that her mistress had not given her any special orders and therefore she did not know what to cook. Jima inquired if no one else had woken up. Chetra replied that they had all gone away looking for Mona's children.

"*Jima!*" exclaimed Mandana. "*You should have kept an eye on those children.*"

"*If you are so concerned, why didn't you look after them?*" blurted out Jima.

"*But they are your grandchildren,*" said Mandana in a shocked tone.

"*I don't believe that biological links make us responsible for our children or grandchildren,*" retorted Jima. "*When there are no feelings, there can be no responsibility.*"

The Clinging Suitor

Jima and Mandana did not touch the *dal*, as it was much too pungent for them. They decided to have some yoghurt and fruit instead for lunch. Sebastian joined them shortly afterwards. He obviously did not feel that he should spend more than an hour searching for Som and Kouros especially since they were Karl's offspring. However, even he displayed more concern than Jima. Since he had not had enough time to eat breakfast, he heartily ate the *dal* and rice. While he was eating, Jima scolded him for his length of stay:

"How come you are still in our palace? You came here to ask Mandana's hand, and she rejected it. Why aren't you leaving now?"

Sebastian was taken back by such a pointed comment. He had dealt with Asians before and had always taken advantage of their generosity, and none of his hosts be they Arab, Persian or Indian had ever withdrawn their invitation or sent him away, no matter how long he had overstayed his welcome. Jima had never adhered to the Iranian code of manners, and was herself an expert in taking advantage of the kindness of people. But she could not stand people who behaved just like her.

Sebastian turned to Mandana hoping that she would come to his defence. Mandana was feeling a little awkward. She also wanted Sebastian to leave and she had told him once before to do so, but she had not the bluntness of her aunt. She just got up and said:

"I am worried for the children; I am going to help with the search." She then turned to Sebastian, *"Don't feel obliged to wait for me, as the search may take hours. So if I don't see you upon my return, have a safe journey back to Delhi."*

Sebastian was dumbfounded. He did not know what to say. He mechanically got up and hugged Mandana, and Mandana left.

Jima was not letting Sebastian out of her eye sight. She stared at him with an irked expression. Sebastian turned to Jima and said:

"Thank you very much for having me, Madam. I am not going to abuse your hospitality further. Could I possibly use your telephone to book a car?"

"Young man, since you have realised that you have abused our hospitality, I am going to give you a tip regarding your transport: Ask Chetra to help you. She can manage to get a rickshaw for you quickly. There might not be any flights from the airport today, but surely you should be able to catch a flight in Srinagar or Simla, provided you leave on the spot."

"Madam, your kindness is unmatched," answered Sebastian. *"And now if you will excuse me."*

He left the room without displaying any emotions. Jima indulged in the sense of satisfaction she extracted from that interaction, smiled emitting the shrill sound of an aborted rooster to express her satisfaction, and then called Chetra to bring her some tea.

In the evening all the family except Jima gathered in the drawing room. Jima had decided to have an early dinner and avoid any further scenes of tears and lamentations. Sebastian – who had yet to leave – joined Mandana's family. He went towards Mandana as soon as he saw her speaking to Sima. Since Sima had invited him to *Ganjbaran* and she did not get along with Jima, he was hoping to take advantage of the situation and see his sojourn extended for another day.

"Mandana," he said, *"Forgive me for imposing myself on you and your family an additional day, but I wasn't able to secure transport this afternoon. I shall be leaving tomorrow with the first available plane. There seems to be one leaving early tomorrow afternoon. I know that your aunt asked me to leave today, but it was virtually impossible."*

"But which aunt?" asked Sima in a surprised tone. *"This is my palace and I should certainly not be so ungracious towards my guests. You are welcome to stay as long as you wish."*

"Thank you, Madam," said Sebastian. *"Your kindness has no bounds."*

"Since you have now been granted unlimited leave to remain in this palace," said Mandana, *"I request that you don't leave tomorrow afternoon. Spend another couple of days here. I am sure that the air of Kashmir is going to rejuvenate your soul."*

Mandana and Sima left the drawing room and Sebastian followed them. He was a bit puzzled and inquired:

"But I thought that you yourself were planning to leave soon?"

Sima took to Sebastian's question and proceeded:

"And yes, when is it exactly that you are leaving Mandana? I thought that you and Jima were leaving today. Not that I want you to leave, but I remember you saying ..."

"As Sebastian said," interrupted Mandana, *"there were no planes available today. We are indeed leaving tomorrow, and I am afraid that if Sebastian flies on the same plane as us, Jima is going to strangle him."*

"But you would certainly not let her," said Sebastian.

"You bet I would," retorted Mandana.

"I wish I were as carefree as all of you," said Sima. *"Even if this were not my palace, I couldn't have possibly left Mona in this state and condition. The poor woman needs all the help we can give her to find her children. My sister must really have a heart of rock, as she evidently doesn't care about her daughter's wellbeing. What have we done to her except show her kindness, to deserve all this bitterness? Mandana, good luck with her."*

Sima went to the kitchen while Mandana walked towards the door to the garden. Sebastian pursued, her trying to carry on the conversation, begging her to take him along on the plane, but Mandana was now disconnected from her surroundings. Sima's last sentence had preoccupied her a little. She thought to herself if Jima is so selfish and vile as to ignore the pain of her own flesh and blood, how could she ever appreciate any other living being? Why should she care about Jima at all? She thought she should use Jima to prevent Maxime form pursuing her, and once in London ditch her in some hotel and vanish. Mandana suddenly turned to Sebastian and said:

"Please be a gentleman Sebastian, and leave me alone. My family has enough problems as such. My aunt Sima has offered you to stay here as much as you please, therefore you don't need to take the same plane as us. I suggest you don't abuse her kindness, and leave a day after us."

"But Mandana...," implored Sebastian.

Mandana interjected:

"Perhaps I have not been clear enough. I am neither interested in marrying you, nor sleeping with you, Sebastian. If you don't stop pursuing me, I will be left with no option other to enlist my family to have you thrown out of this place immediately. So please retain some of whatever dignity you have left, and keep away from me."

This time Sebastian realised that there was no hope of conquering Mandana. Although he was deeply hurt, he kept his emotions to himself. As a child he was constantly told by the menfolk around him, such as his father and school teachers, that a man never cries, and therefore he had always avoided shedding tears and demonstrating his feelings. He went towards Chetra and asked if she could call him a rickshaw from the village. She replied that it was a bit too late to call her cousin as in the evening it was too difficult to go anywhere. The young man insisted on being taken to the village. Chetra, who was aware of Sebastian's interest in Mandana, realised what must have happened and sympathised with him. She advised Sebastian to spend the night in the palace and said her cousin would pick him up early in the morning with his rickshaw, and take him wherever he desired. She ended her advice by quoting a famous Indo-Iranian adage 'one night isn't a thousand nights'. Sebastian realised he was making his own life more difficult by leaving right away. Although he was feeling quite low, he followed Chetra's advice, and requested that her cousin fetch him at six in the morning. He then headed to his bedroom and shut the door.

Beauty Does not Lead to the Altar

Mona did not budge from the drawing room. She cried in Karl's arms, until he decided to go out and continue with the search. Bahram and his sons followed him. Mona continued crying and Sima and Azar stayed to comfort her.

Mandana entered the room and said:

"By no means do I want to let Mona down. However, I think that by taking Jima away with me tomorrow, I will be lifting a heavy weight from your shoulders."

As she finished her sentence, Chetra came in and said that two policemen were waiting in the main hallway. Sima turned to Azar and Mona, and said:

"I contacted the authorities before dinner - we obviously need help with the search."

She then left the drawing room and asked Chetra to follow her, since Sima needed her to act as interpreter.

Once Sima left, a still tearful Mona said with a quivering voice:

"I remember the time I was complaining about having young children. I said they were the cause of wrinkles on women's faces, and look to what have I been reduced. I'm being punished for my ingratitude at motherhood. I did not value my children enough, and now it's too late to repent."

And she continued sobbing. Azar attempted to comfort her relative:

"Mona dear, we all complain about our children and husbands. Don't torture yourself by reminding yourself of insignificant utterances that belong to the past, and are certainly out of context."

"But you know how unlucky I have been," continued Mona. *"When I was still quite young, my mother's mental health severely deteriorated after the loss of*

my older sister. I also lost my father at a young age, my husband is unfaithful, and at present it's far from certain that I will ever see my dear children!"

"*You shall, my dear,*" reassured Azar, "*you shall.*"

Mandana was silently and discreetly gazing at the inconsolable mother. She thought that she might have still been jealous of Mona, had she not had a brief liaison with her husband. However, her fleeting romantic encounter confirmed to her that actually she needed – for it was a need, indeed - something more than sensual and sexual titilation and aesthetic gratification that a handsome fit man such as Mona's husband seemed able to provide. On the other hand, she had difficulty feeling much empathy with Mona. This was not out of cold-heartedness, for she could certainly see that Mona was beside herself with anxiety about the disappearance of her children, but out of a conviction that their disappearance was to be only temporary. Although Mandana had realised that beauty was not everything, she still believed that looks were telling. To her, Mona was really not that pleasant a person to look at. She thought that none of the other female members of her family were as plain-looking.

She suddenly decided to leave the drawing room and enter the reception room where a wall-to-wall mirror was hanging. She looked in the mirror admiring herself. She recalled silently all the compliments she had ever received. An old Greek man had once told her that she was the reincarnation of the magnificent Roxana with whom Alexander of Macedonia had fallen in love twenty-three centuries ago during his conquest of Persia. A young Syrian man had once told her that her eyes were as perfect as purple Libyan grapes. A middle-aged Armenian man had told her that her skin bore the pink colour of water lily petals. Her smile suddenly faded when she thought of her own luck. Despite her father's wealth, and her beauty, she remained a singleton. She then thought that perhaps once she had acquired her diploma in New York, men would flock to marry her, as they would not just lust for her, but would value her for her professional potentials.

While she was still looking at herself in the mirror, Mona entered the room and said in a sad tone:

"*If I were as beautiful as you, I would have also spent a lot of time admiring myself in the mirror.*"

Mandana was suddenly startled, and thought of Mona's comments suspiciously, lest they were indicative of her envy and her efforts to cast over her the 'evil eye' - she replied:

"Oh, I don't think I am really that beautiful. My nose is slightly too big and I am thinking of having surgery."

"Don't be silly. There is nothing wrong with your nose. I know many women who have had their nose re-done; they might have now the perfect nose, but they don't look pretty any more. I have a beautiful Iranian friend in London who did not like a small bump on her nose. She had it removed, but lost all her Oriental charm. Most of the time we had better leave things to Mother Nature. Just look at all these huge ugly man-made cities. We have ruined nature in order to have well-structured buildings. Were I as beautiful as you, Karl wouldn't have cheated on me, and I wouldn't have come here and have my children gone missing."

Mona's last sentence made Mandana even more uncomfortable, as she was now convinced that Mona had cast the evil eye over her, and that, consequently, something bad was going to happen to her. She thought quickly and responded:

"Mona dear, Karl could have had the most beautiful wife on the earth, he would still have cheated on her. Infidelity is part of his nature. I know that it's a very difficult situation to be in, but you can look at your marriage from another angle. Karl could have married any woman, but he chose you. Clearly, there is something special about you – be it some virtue or feature of your personality – that attracted him to you, and not another woman. I would love to know how you met him, and how you enchanted him, though I am by no means surprised that you did so, or any other man, for that matter."

Mona thought for a few seconds and said:

"It was at a reception at our aunt Atoossa's villa in the outskirts of Rome. I was then an undergraduate in London, and my mother barely gave me enough money for nice clothes or even going to a hairdresser. That night I was wearing a simple black dress our aunt Atoossa had given me as a present along with a pair of little diamond earrings given to me by our grandfather. The reception room was quite crowded. There were about a hundred people. I saw a handsome man from afar talking to an old classmate of our aunt. She was a lovely Italian lady, who has sadly now passed away. She knew me as I had seen her at aunt Atoossa's in the past. She was quite glad to see me, and introduced me to Karl and told him that

I also lived in London. I couldn't help smiling at him, and, Karl smiled back at me. Despite the fact that we were surrounded by many beautiful girls with lavish dresses, Karl spent the whole night conversing with me. I believe he preferred talking to me than to spending time with the other girls, as I stood out from them with my simplicity."

"How had Karl ended up in Rome?" asked Mandana.

"He was then friends with one of our distant cousins Fereydoun, and he had invited him to stay at our aunt Atoossa's place. This allowed me to spend two entire days with him."

Mandana looked at Mona and said:

"You see, my dear cousin - I have never had such a marvellous opportunity, and yet you envy me; why can't you appreciate your good fortune?"

"But what good fortune? asked Mona. *"I have lost my two children who are the only things that bind me and Karl together. Don't you understand that I have a husband who doesn't really care about me? He hardly shows me any affection."*

And once again Mona burst into tears.

Mona, despite resenting Mandana's comments that caused her to erupt, was still hoping that her cousin would take her into motherly bosom and embrace her to console her. Yet Mona's anecdote about her first encounter with Karl had silenced Mandana into reflection so deep that, quite unintentionally, she became totally oblivious to a crying mother's emotional need for the reassurance that an embrace may impart.

Mandana was not concerned about the way Mona's marriage had evolved. She still envied Mona for the excitement she should have experienced the day she had met an eligible bachelor at her aunt's reception, and in addition had the opportunity to stay under the same roof for a couple of days to get better acquainted. She then thought to herself:

"Why on earth at a reception filled with beauties, would Karl be attracted to - what she considered Mona to be - the least attractive woman? Was it that Karl was looking for an easily malleable compliant virgin? Mona would have surely fulfilled those criteria at the time. Or was it that Mona was extremely shrewd and knew how to seduce men?"

For Mandana the latter seemed more plausible as Karl could have surely found a woman to fit those criteria but who was also beautiful had he gone to the East to marry and then return to his life in the West. With her thoughts about Mona potentially being more than meets the eye still churning in her mind, she glanced at her without being able to suppress her momentary mistrust and aversion. This happened just at the moment Mona had looked back at her and had caught her gaze. Mandana then ran to the kitchen to find wild rue seeds. Mona remained seated crying incessantly.

Chetra had gone to sleep and therefore Mandana had no choice but to search for the seeds herself. After ten minutes she found them in a sealed jar, and burned them on the stove to protect herself against her cousin's evil eye. Reassured by the noise of the burning seeds and the sight of their smoke, she shut the stove and went to her bedroom confidently, with a serene smile. Although she had enjoyed her stay at *Ganjbaran*, she was henceforth looking forward to her new adventure, which she hoped would begin the following morning.

A DISTURBING REVELATION

The following morning at six o'clock, Chetra's cousin arrived with his rickshaw to fetch Sebastian. He left without anybody seeing or hearing him. An hour later, Mandana got out of bed and hurried to Jima's room to wake her up, as she knew how it could take her aunt up to two hours to prepare given how she never rushed for anybody nor was concerned about the possibility of holding others up. Mandana told her that the car to the airport was due to arrive at nine o'clock in the morning.

Mandana got ready faster than usual as she did not feel like applying any make-up. She went to the kitchen to prepare some packed lunch for the trip. She took an entire box of tangerines from the walk-in larder beside the kitchen and emptied it into a bag. She washed five apples for the journey. She peeled a couple of mangoes and diced them in such a way that they would fit in a plastic container. As she put on the samovar to boil, Chetra arrived with a batch of fresh *naans*. Mandana asked her how she had managed to make a round trip to the village so early and quickly. Chetra replied that she had not left *Ganjbaran* as there was no need to do so – some time ago she had discovered a tandoor oven under the small arched structure in the garden, and she had decided to use it that morning to make *naan* bread. Mandana said that she was impressed with her skills. Chetra said that there was nothing admirable about her baking expertise as all the women in her village knew how to make *naan*.

Mandana sat down in the breakfast room to have some tea with the fresh bread, cheese and cucumbers when Azar, Bahram, and Karl entered the room. Mandana greeted them. Azar and Bahram greeted her back, but Karl ignored her. Mandana was not offended as she was by that stage past caring – she thought him and his behaviour to be childish.

"*It's another beautiful and sunny day,*" she said. "*I am sure it's going to be difficult for all of you to return to your cloudy cities. By the way, any progress with the search?*"

"*Unfortunately, not,*" Azar replied. "*We are going to continue today. The sunny weather will console us a little. All this sunshine reminds me of Tehran. Bahram, we should really think of moving to a sunnier place. The idea of returning to rainy Vancouver depresses me.*"

"*For the moment,*" said Bahram, "*don't worry about returning to Vancouver, we have more important things to worry about.*"

"*I am sorry, Karl,*" said Azar. "*I am sure we are going to find Som and Kouros today. The police said eight of their men will be joining us this morning for the search.*" Azar then turned to Mandana, "*Aren't you leaving today?*"

"*Yes, indeed.*" replied Mandana, "*We will be leaving in a couple of hours or so.*"

"*Oh my,*" sighed Azar. "*I always find it difficult to part with families and friends, especially after the Revolution. We no longer know when we'll be seeing each other again. We are all scattered around the world.*"

Upstairs, Mona was feeling nauseous. Although she wanted to believe that her children would be found, she was beginning to lose faith. Intuitively she felt that there was a further disaster looming. She left her bedroom with dishevelled hair and a long creased dress hoping she would come across some other soul who would comfort her. She was hesitating to go downstairs as she was dreading any further bad news. She stood outside her bedroom for a couple of minutes, until she saw Sima leave her room. Sima quickly went towards her niece and took hold of her hands.

"*Mona, you really look pale. You should perhaps stay in bed.*"

"*I am feeling too sick to stay in bed. I need some fresh air, but I haven't the energy to go outside by myself.*"

"*You can't go out like this,*" said Sima. "*Let me grab a jacket for you, otherwise you will catch a cold.*"

She came back with a jacket and took Mona downstairs to the garden.

Sima put her left arm around Mona's shoulders and walked beside her. She told her not to worry further,

"*Your children are going to be with you today.*"

"*If my children were to be found, they would have been found already yester-day. I think something terrible has happened to them.*"

"*Don't say these things. You are just tired and worried, and I understand why you are feeling like this right now. I am sure your children are just lost somewhere in the forest. This isn't a big city where there are child abusers who molest and kill. Nobody would harm your children here.*"

"*Sima dear,*" said Mona, "*I appreciate your efforts to make me feel better. I am also convinced that there are no perverts nearby. However, in the forest there are wild animals which are as capable of hurting my children as much as a sadistic monster in London. I really want to believe that I will find my children, but I am not able to do so. This is why I am no longer able to weep any more. I am in too much pain.*"

Sima hugged Mona as strongly as she could. She then told her that they should go and have something to eat. Mona said that she had no appetite, but Sima insisted on taking her to the kitchen, where Azar was waiting for them.

Azar's sons were also in the kitchen having breakfast. Bahram and Karl were already gone to continue their search, while Mandana made her way back upstairs. Azar and her sons bade the two ladies good morning. Mona greeted them back but did not pursue any conversation. She remained silent. Azar was also concerned about Mona, and was trying to reassure her that they would find her sons.

Sima asked Azar if Mandana and Jima had already left.

"*Mandana just had breakfast with us,*" informed Azar, "*but we have seen neither Jima nor Sebastian.*"

Jima was taking her time to dress up, and her slow pace was mak-ing Mandana anxious. At nine o'clock, Mandana went to Jima's room and reminded her that the car was bound to be at *Ganjbaran* any time in the next few minutes:

"*If you are not ready by then, I will leave without you.*"

Jima got upset at Mandana and blurted out:

"*Instead of giving your aunt ultimatums, you had better take my suitcases downstairs.*"

Not long after, the car from the airport arrived and stopped in front of the palace. Mandana had only one suitcase, as she had decided to leave behind most of her cosmetics and unnecessary clothes she had brought to India. Jima, on the other hand, was clinging to her belongings. She had also purchased many silk and pashmina shawls whenever she was transiting from an Indian city to *Ganjbaran*.

The previous day, Mandana had got worried when she had seen Jima's four suitcases in addition to her three big hand-bags. She had secretly removed more than a quarter of Jima's belongings, making sure that she was not throwing away any expensive clothes. She had then offered Chetra to take anything left behind in the annex room, where she had repacked Jima's belongings. Chetra was delighted.

In the morning, as Chetra was helping Mandana take the suitcase downstairs, Jima noticed that two of her hand bags were missing and that the one she was carrying was very light. She asked Mandana if she had forgotten the other two upstairs, and Mandana explained that she had squeezed all her belongings into the four suitcases. Had Jima picked one of her suitcases she would have also realised how light they had become. Mandana had left two of the suitcases half empty so that Jima would not notice the missing items until she had reached Delhi, as once away from *Ganjbaran*, Jima could not claim her belongings. Jima only made sure that the handbag which contained her jewels was intact and went to the garden.

Mandana went quickly to the kitchen to bid Mona farewell. She did not say much to her in order not to keep the car waiting. As she hugged Mona, she could feel the cold frailness of her body, which worried her. Mona's body temperature had dropped dramatically. Mona was too weak even to express how she felt. Mandana parted from Mona, hoping that Sima and Azar would take care of her.

Sima had conveniently gone to search for Mona's children in order to avoid seeing Jima again. Azar was the only member of the family who saw Mandana and Jima to the car in order to wish them a safe journey. She thought that Sebastian was travelling with them. As she did not see him, she asked Mandana and Jima where he was. Although Mandana had wanted to satisfy Azar's curiosity, she did not know the answer:

"*He has probably left earlier in the morning for Srinagar.*"

Azar hugged Mandana and Jima, and invited them to visit her in Vancouver. Mandana said that she hoped that Mona's children would be found soon and that all of them would be able to relax and enjoy the paradise that was *Ganjbaran*.

As Mandana and Jima sat in the car, Jima began criticising Sima for ignoring them and being a cold-hearted woman. Mandana did not let Jima continue vilifying Sima:

"*I am sorry Jima, but we couldn't say much better things about you. Your daughter's children disappeared and you appear incapable of expressing any sympathy. Worse even: you were responsible for what had happened, and you showed no remorse.*"

Jima wanted to interrupt Mandana, but she did not let her:

"*You did not even appear to care about how your daughter felt. You did not hold her in your arms, when she needed you the most. Didn't you see in what state the poor woman was? What are you: a piece of rock, with no emotions and sensitivity?*"

Jima got very angry at Mandana's comments and shouted:

"*How dare you judge me?*"

"*I have every right to judge you,*" thundered Mandana. "*You have been relying on me ever since we found the jewels to help you with your trips and future plans. You were even thinking of living with me, as you were afraid of being left alone by yourself. Nobody in the family likes you, and have you ever wondered why? I don't anymore. The last few weeks have been very telling. You are devoid of any human feelings. How could a mother be so mean to her daughter?*"

"*You can't judge a person if you don't know their history.*"

"*Oblige me by telling me,*" snarled Mandana, "*as sincerely I don't wish to continue my trip with you after we land in New Delhi.*"

Jima was suddenly petrified by the prospect of finding herself alone in Delhi. She burst into tears and lamented:

"*Life has been so unfair to me. I lost my beautiful daughter when I was a young woman, and was widowed quite young…*"

Mandana was not affected at all by Jima's tears and said forcefully:

"*Many people lose their loved ones, but they don't lose their heart and soul. Nothing can justify your behaviour. In addition, everybody in the family says that you did not love your husband. Therefore, his death couldn't have affected you that much. At the time you were in Iran, surrounded by your family who gave you all the support you needed. In addition, you still had another child – Mona – for whom you had to care. But no, you surely didn't. With your behaviour in the last few days I could imagine how deserted that poor woman must have felt as a child.*"

Jima's tears suddenly stopped and she howled:

"People should be grateful that I did not strangle Mona. She is the one who should have died instead of Anahita. My little daughter was so beautiful. She had lips redder than morello cherries, her teeth were like pearls, her skin was soft and pink like a lotus, her hair was shiny and black like a crow's feathers. She was the most beautiful girl on earth. When she died I was left with this ugly and clumsy girl, of whom I felt ashamed. I had become the laughing stock of friends and neighbours. A couple of neighbours had said that their god had taken away my beautiful daughter and left me with an ugly one to punish me for my polytheism. Our family always had faith in gods, and none had experienced my agony. What had I done wrong? My life had indeed changed ever since Mona was born. She's brought me misfortune. I lost both Anahita and my husband, and this Medusa lived on to become a source of pain. She should have died, but she lived. I wasn't able to kill her, and yet people say that I am evil."

Mandana was horrified by what she had heard. She now felt even more sorry for Mona. She really did not wish to continue the trip with Jima. She was disturbed and disoriented at the same time, and needed to feel the presence of a relative or friend.

Remedies Against a Worthless Husband

Throughout the morning, Azar looked after Mona. She was hoping to make her eat, but to no avail. By the time Sima came back for lunch, Mona had lost consciousness. Sima and Azar took her temperature and got worried. Sima asked Chetra if there was a physician at her village who could assist them. Chetra responded that they had a very competent healer, who cured everyone. She then called the main shop of her village and asked a lady there to locate the healer and ask him to come to *Ganjbaran*.

A couple of hours later, while Azar was sitting beside Mona and stroking her hair, the men of the family arrived in a subdued mood. Azar took them as far as possible from the drawing room where Mona was lying, and then allowed them to speak.

Bahram reported that the police had found Som's jacket torn with sticky purple stains:

"They said that they can't help us with our search as they are convinced the children have been eaten by some wild animals."

Azar turned to Karl and inquired:

"What are you planning to do now?"

"I saw the jacket and the stains..." replied Karl. *"I don't think there is much hope. We can't spend the rest of our lives here."*

"Aren't we losing hope too soon?" asked Azar.

"Had you seen the pieces of clothes, you would have given up hope too," answered Karl.

"Oh please Karl, we can't give up hope," said Azar.

"I can't keep on staying like this here and hoping. I need to move on."

143

Karl then called Chetra and asked her if she had the number of the airport at hand.

As Karl was speaking with an employee at the airport, a rickshaw arrived at the palace. Chetra went to the garden to greet her cousin and the healer. She ushered them in and asked her cousin to sit and wait in the hallway. She then led the healer to the drawing room where Sima was attending to Mona. Chetra introduced the healer as Bhaktijee.

Chetra had to act as an interpreter, for Bhaktijee only spoke Kashmiri. Bhaktijee took Mona's pulse. He then rolled up her sleeves and dropped some kind of pastel green oil on the middle of her arm, and squeezed a drop of cobalt blue oil on her palm. After forty seconds both drops turned yellow. He then held both of Mona's hands tightly and released them. Then, Bhaktijee spoke for about five minutes and Chetra translated his words succinctly to tell her family that the healer felt that Mona was 'dying emotionally'. They were advised to act immediately as Mona had been suffering from a lack of affection. Bhaktijee said that Mona had not been loved during her childhood, and the lack of affection from her husband, and the loss of her children were too much for her to bear. Sima interrupted Chetra and said:

"*Is Bhaktijee speaking metaphorically? Her husband is still alive, and it's far from certain that her children are not. I don't think it's her relation with her husband that has reduced her to such a state – it seems to be her losing hope in finding her children.*"

Chetra translated Sima's comments for Bhaktijee, but Bhaktijee was still adamant that Mona would never see her children again, and her husband was soon to disappear from her life. Sima interrupted again:

"*Is Bhaktijee here to heal Mona or to read her fortune?*"

Chetra said that Bhaktijee had divinatory powers, which allowed him to heal people holistically. As Chetra was about to finish her sentence, Karl came in the drawing room and announced his departure. He said that since Mona was in good hands in *Ganjbaran*, there was no need for her to accompany him back to London. He said that he had miraculously been able to secure a seat on the plane to Delhi, and since a rickshaw was already there, he was going to leave on the spot. While Azar and Sima looked at him with evident concern, the telephone rang and Sima went to answer.

Azar and Karl hugged and bid each other farewell. Karl then knelt in front of the sofa on which Mona was lying and held her hand. He told her that he was leaving earlier as he found the atmosphere of the palace too suffocating:

"*I am sure that you are going to recover soon and return to London in no time.*"

Mona did not even turn her head to look at Karl. She remained motionless. Karl kissed her hand and left the room. Chetra just commented that Bhaktijee might be upset if he was kept a few hours longer at the palace, and therefore she did not think it was right for Karl to travel on her cousin's rickshaw to the airport. Karl replied arrogantly that he was bound to miss his flight otherwise, and should have the priority:

"*Bhaktijee lives just half an hour from here. Should worst come to worst, you can walk him back.*"

As Karl was leaving the room, Sima came back from the phone call aghast. Karl wanted to hug her and say good-bye, but she stopped him.

"*It was Mandana,*" she announced. "*She is at the airport and is going to be with us in an hour. She refused to tell me what had gone wrong and where Jima was during her call.*"

"*Your transportation problem is now solved then,*" said Karl to Chetra. "*So you no longer need to worry for Bhaktijee.*"

Sima censured Karl:

"*Explain to me this, Karl: how can it be that men are capable of leaving their wives at times when they know that their spouses need them the most?*"

"*Sima, this is typical feminist, anti-male rhetoric,*" retorted Karl, "*and I really don't have time to get entangled in it. All I can say is that you shouldn't judge others without knowledge of the full facts. Good-bye.*"

Karl left the room and Sima did not even bother reply.

Meanwhile, Bhaktijee had gone to the kitchen with Chetra. Bhaktijee finished preparing a concoction of seeds and herbal oil with nine drops of honey, and returned to the room to give it to Mona. He pressed softly above Mona's jaws, in order to feed her a concoction. As she finished drinking, she began coughing. Five minutes later she was once again conscious of her surroundings. Bhaktijee then asked Chetra to bring a metal container along with a tray and some small pieces of wood. He dropped some leaves, seeds and the pieces of wood in the container and lit them by throwing shiny seeds on them. Azar, Sima and Mona were enchanted. He brought the container close to Mona's face so that she could inhale some smoke. He chanted a few mantras and displayed his tongue so that Mona would understand that she should put out her tongue. Bhaktijee put some sort of a dried berry on her tongue, and through some gestures conveyed that she should swallow it. A few minutes later Mona was fast asleep.

Bhaktijee said a few sentences and Chetra translated that Bhaktijee was going to leave the necessary amount of seeds, herbs and herbal oils for them to cure Mona. She explained that the smoke of the herbs and the seeds would not only help Mona to recover physically, but also spiritually. She could thus overcome the pain of loss and unrequited love. Bhaktijee said that he would return in a week to check on Mona, as the pain she has had to endure was serious. Chetra then told him that he could not leave right away, as Mona's husband had left with the rickshaw. He replied in an amused tone and Chetra translated for Azar and Sima, that Karl's spirit had already left his wife and the palace yesterday. He then added that he did not mind waiting provided he was allowed to wonder in the garden and collect some plants and herbs. According to him *Ganjbaran* hid special natural resources and gems.

A Sudden End

Bhaktijee did not have much time to wander in the garden, as Mandana was soon brought to the palace with a car followed by a rickshaw. Sima and Azar went out to greet her, while the drivers were taking out the suitcases and a draped body. Then they turned to Mandana and asked where they should leave the lady. Mandana then put the same question to Sima. Sima's jaws dropped wide open:

"*Is this Jima's corpse?*" queried Sima.

"*Yes* –" replied Mandana. "*I am really sorry that you have to get the news in this way.*"

"*What happened?*" asked Azar.

"*Please let these men take the suitcases in and put Jima's body somewhere to lie,*" said Mandana, "*and then I will tell you the story.*"

Sima instructed the men to put Jima on a bench in the porch. As the three women were going inside, Chetra ran behind them and told Sima that Bhaktijee had to leave. She was hinting to Sima that she had to pay his wage. Sima put fifty rupees in an envelope and put a ten rupee note in Chetra's hand saying that the ten rupees was for Bhaktijee's return fare to the village. Before Chetra left, Sima asked her to bring a tray with a pot of tea and *barfis* to the reception hall once she had seen Bhaktijee to the car.

As Mona was asleep in the drawing room, Sima ushered Azar and Mandana to the reception hall. Right when they had seated themselves to listen to Mandana, they heard Bahram calling Azar. Azar said that she could not possibly leave now, and begged Mandana to begin. She finished by saying:

"*Our family should receive an award for keeping its composure, as we have been through a number of dramas in the past few days.*"

147

"*I am sure if we had lost people we really cared for,*" Mandana pointed out, "*we wouldn't have been able to sit calmly here and sip tea. Anyway Jima's death was quite sudden. You remember, Azar, when we left this morning she was perfectly fine. Even in the car, nothing unusual was noticeable. On the way to the airport, we had a little argument over her behaviour towards Mona. Sima's words had affected me, as she had told me that a woman who has no affection for her own daughter can't care for anyone else. Therefore, I conveyed to Jima that her behaviour was unacceptable. Then she told me the most appalling story about how she hated Mona and wished that she had died instead of her second daughter. I was dying to reach Delhi in order not to see Jima's face ever again. After our conversation in the car, we had stopped talking to each other. Until we boarded the small plane, Jima did not display any signs of illness or discomfort. Once the plane took off, the co-pilot came out and asked Jima to fasten her seatbelt. Jima did not respond and seemed to be fast asleep. The man asked me if I could fasten her seatbelt as he did not want to have to wake an old lady. As I was trying to fasten her seat belt, I noticed that she wasn't really breathing and her hands were frigid. I called her three times, and then started to shake her. Jima's head dropped sideways limply. I called the co-pilot, telling him that my aunt seemed dead. Since we had been in the air for less than half an hour and I was the only living passenger, the co-pilot asked me whether I would rather return to our initial airport than go to Delhi. The choice was obvious. I did not have any relatives in Delhi, and therefore I decided to come back.*"

"*Human beings don't want to think of themselves as evil,*" observed Azar. "*I think your last conversation with Jima must have made her realise what a horrible mother she had been to Mona. The poor woman was too old to cope with this reality, and therefore the guilt may well have killed her.*"

"*Oh, please don't say such a thing,*" said Mandana. "*Now you make me feel guilty.*"

"*Don't blame yourself for Jima's death,*" consoled Sima. "*You did not harm her in any way. She was an unhappy woman. Ganjbaran should have been the place where she should have been happiest, being surrounded by her daughter, sister and loved ones, and yet she was ever so miserable. She was suffering from within and was unable to express any affection to another human being – the most invaluable gift one person can offer another. Ganjbaran may have made her realise that life had no meaning to her. At her age, one can't live long if there is nothing to live for."*

Azar shook her head and then said:

"It might not be a little crude to speak about these things at this point, but I wonder to whom she may have left her possessions given how she resented her daughter."

"To no-one," stated Sima. *"Jima didn't like anybody. And, anyway, she had no wealth."*

"Well, she had some fabulous pieces of jewellery," noted Azar. *"You remember the brooch she was wearing?"*

Mandana realised that she had to interfere right away before the rest of the family set claims to the jewels Jima had taken from the pit:

"Azar dear, that brooch belonged to me. I had just lent it to Jima as she was desperate to show off to Sima. You remember, Sebastian had given it to me."

"I can't believe this story for a second," said Sima. *"I saw that young man. He did not seem to be the type to give such gifts. He seemed to have been very much after your money. That brooch comes from somewhere else."*

"Wherever it comes from Sima, it's mine. As you said it yourself, Jima had no money."

With these words Mandana left the room.

Jima's Heir

While walking away, Mandana remembered that half of the money they had received in Kuwait was in a separate account in Jima's name. Legally the only person entitled to this was Mona. Although Mandana was convinced that she, herself, was the rightful owner of that money, she knew that the banks would turn down her claim. She went into the garden and looked at the sky. She thought to herself that perhaps there is justice in this world. Mona had suffered a lot throughout her life. She had a traumatising childhood with Jima as her mother. She married a man who cheated on her, and now she had lost her children. Perhaps the seventeen and a half million pounds were the gods' present to soothe her pain. She therefore decided to reveal the existence of Jima's fortune to Mona, but she did not know when. She had to invent a story however, to hide Jima's source of wealth. She definitely did not want Sima to know about the money, as then she would have to deal with a long inquisition, that might lead to her being forced to give Sima the gems she had found. She decided that she would wait for Mona to leave *Ganjbaran* before sharing the information. Mandana then thought that if Karl discovered his wife's wealth, he might decide to con her. Moreover the children had now vanished, and there was not much to keep the couple together. But then that was up to Mona. If she was not smart enough to know her husband by now, then there was nothing much she could do about it.

A Housewife Will Always Be Her Husband's Shadow

Before Sima and Azar went in different directions, Azar said:
"Sima! Bhaktijee has indeed divinatory powers. He had already stated that Karl was leaving Mona. Before knowing the facts, I thought he was speaking metaphorically too. Do you think he can tell us about our own future?"

By the time Bahram found his wife, he was quite upset:
"I have been calling you in the past thirty minutes, and looking for you everywhere. Why didn't you answer?"

"I am sorry Bahram. Mandana just returned with Jima's dead body, and that was a shock to me and Sima. I couldn't have possibly left them in that state of mourning and come to you."

"I am sure they are not really that distressed. Neither of them really liked that old woman. She had been really mean to Sima before she left."

"I know," replied Azar, *"but nonetheless, it was a shock as it was quite unexpected. We were also pondering on how to announce the news to Mona. We know that Jima did not like her, but again she was her mother. The poor woman has been through a lot lately and we don't know how she will cope with another painful news."*

After hearing Azar, Bahram calmed down and said:
"I think it's time for us to leave as well. Karl and Mona seem to have given up the search, and the police believes that they have been eaten by some wild beast. In these conditions, there is no way we can find them. Our children have to go back to school, and I have to go back to work."

151

"But I feel bad leaving Mona behind in such a state."

"She has Sima to look after her."

"Allright," said Azar submissively. *"Check with the airline and let me know when I should start packing."*

———

During the dinner, Mandana was asked to give details of the incident once again. Mandana did not mind retelling the story, as she thought there was something extraordinary about Jima's sudden death. Azar then probed Sima regarding her plans with the corpse.

"Jima always wanted to be cremated," said Sima. *"I am so happy for her that she passed away in India as I believe there is nowhere better to be cremated than here."*

"You should act quickly as it isn't very wise to keep a corpse for long on the porch of your palace," recommended Bahram.

Azar then turned to Mandana:

"How long are you planning to stay now in Ganjbaran?"

"I am not so sure any more," replied Mandana. *"It has been a long and difficult day. I have never had anyone passing away beside me. My mind is slightly unsettled and I believe I will need two or three days to recuperate from the incident before I can think about making future plans."*

As she finished her sentence, the telephone rang. Sima asked Chetra to answer. As Chetra left the room to answer the phone, Mandana said to Azar:

"It's really good to have you at Ganjbaran. You and your family have given life to the palace. I hope that you are not going to leave soon."

"We are hoping to leave with the next available flight," interrupted Bahram.

It was as if cold water had been poured on Sima. She was very saddened by the news, as Azar had been the only supportive relative throughout the family crisis. Suddenly tears rolled down her cheeks. Azar was about to say something, but Chetra interrupted the scene and said that Maxime has called to speak with Mandana.

Mandana left the room and Azar got up to sit beside Sima. She told her not to cry as she was sure that they were going to meet again soon.

Ganjbaran

"*There is such a long distance between Vancouver and Ganjbaran,*" said Sima. "*I doubt that we will be able to see each other any time soon.*"

"*Our future visits have not been set in stone,*" observed Azar. "*Who knows where you will be living in two or three years. Once Mandana and Mona are gone, you might not wish to stay in Ganjbaran.*"

Sima had not thought about this. Initially, she had come to *Ganjbaran* for some peace, but this was mainly due to the shock of the revolution and its aftermath. Now she had realised that for her well-being she needed to be surrounded by her family. Back in Iran she had never had any time on her own, as her relatives were always around. This was why she searched a distant retreat. Her few days of solitude before Jima's arrival in *Ganjbaran* were enough to make her understand that there was nothing more depressing than an isolated residence. Even the beauty of the palace and the landscape around it could not make up for the absence of her relatives.

The Right Formula to Conquer a Man

After they had finished dinner, Sima asked Chetra who they should contact in her village to help with the cremation. She also asked whether she thought it was normal that Mona had not opened her eyes since Bhaktijee had left. Chetra told her not to worry and that it was the effect of the potion that Bhaktijee had given Mona, and that she would wake up in the morning feeling much better.

Sima went to the drawing room to check on Mona and saw Mandana in the room. She asked her niece in a very soft voice:

"*How is she?*"

"*We won't be able to tell until she wakes up,*" whispered Mandana. "*All I can say is that at least she's alive.*"

"*Let's leave her in peace then.*"

Both women left the room and went to the reception hall. Sima then asked:

"*How serious is your relation with Maxime?*"

Mandana laughed and said:

"*What kind of a story have you made up in your mind? Maxime is the manager of the Swissair office in New Delhi. I contacted him to book tickets and hotels in Delhi. Since I had not shown up he wanted to know what he should do.*"

"*Did you reschedule your flight then?*"

"*I did not. I am not going to leave you in this situation, alone with Mona. Did Karl say that he is divorcing her?*"

Suddenly Sima remembered Bhaktijee's words, but she decided not to expose her source and act as she were herself an oracle:

"Karl did not say anything, but it's quite obvious that he plans on divorcing Mona. I only hope that he isn't going to wait until Mona has returned to London to announce it to her. She would be all alone in London and might not be able to handle the news by herself. I think we should advise him to tell her over the phone while Mona is still with us."

"Why are you so certain that Karl wants to leave her?" inquired Mandana. *"You are the one who insised that she mustn't give up on him so soon as he must have loved her sufficiently to marry her. Though we doubt his feelings for her today, I am interested to know what has made you change your mind on his account?"*

"I always wish to give people the benefit of the doubt," said Sima. *"Before meeting Karl I truly believed that Mona should give her marriage a second chance, but since I saw the way he treated her and witnessed his apetite for other women, I sincerely believe that there is no hope for this marriage. We don't know how long Karl's affairs have lasted, and he is clearly not attracted to Mona any more. Now that the children have disappeared, there is virtually nothing keeping them together."*

Mandana felt a little ill at ease, as she wondered if Sima knew anything about her fling with Karl. Otherwise, how could she have 'witnessed Karl's apetite for other women', for clearly there was no other beautiful woman in the palace, except for Mandana of course. The young woman decided to ignore Sima's insinuation and said:

"There are so many couples who have no children and live, if not happily, bearably together. Surely he couldn't have left his wife suddenly without good cause. He couldn't possibly leave her now that she needs him the most."

"Mandana dear," said Sima, *"I thought that you had sufficient experience of men. Most love affairs begin and end on a whim. Couples who can't appreciate each other physically, emotionally, spiritually, and above all have difficulty communicating are bound to split. And most couples get together without considering these matters at the outset. It's clear to me that Karl no longer appreciates Mona in any of these ways. As you rightly believe, he shouldn't leave Mona at a time when she is at her most desperate and inconsolable, but unfortunately, he has. He dumped her in India and in cowardly fashion went back to England, running away from his spousal responsibilities and leaving poor Mona behind."*

Mandana was very much affected by Sima's words, as she had always been dreaming of finding a handsome, professional young man who would love and cherish her, and support her throughout her life.

"Is it only children that bind a man to his wife?"

"It usually is," replied Sima. *"Have you not seen how many women get themselves pregnant to keep a man?"*

"Yes. But I found that to be so dishonest and pathetic at the same time. Don't you want a man to really love you for who you are, and for him to be with you for that reason?"

"How naïve of you, darling," replied Sima. *"Yes, that would have been ideal, but you must realise, surely, by now, that the ideal is far from the real. I want that ideal too, but I have paid the price for that pursuit - that's why I am a single woman. Most women who get themselves knocked-up do it for financial reasons. They want to trap a man from whom they can extract some financial gain. You and I can't fall in this category – we may want to feel that we are too principled to do so, but actually we are too proud and we both refuse to humble ourselves. We refuse to shed tears in front of men even if the mere act could save our relationship."*

"But I have seen women who got themselves pregnant from good-looking and younger men who clearly don't have much money."

"You are wrong Mandana. These younger, handsome men have not only their youth and beauty to offer, they have also good professional prospects – a future, basically. If you look closely, these women don't run after handsome drug addicts, they really choose their mates."

"It never crossed my mind to calculate what I wanted from a man before dating him. I was certainly hoping that one of them would love me and marry me, but all of them wanted only to sleep with me."

"If your aim was to get married, then why did you sleep with all these men who clearly did not want to marry you? Perhaps you have not been absolutely honest with yourself. Maybe you should admit to yourself that your biological urges are too strong."

At that point, Mandana did not know what to say. Again she just pondered on her brief affair with Karl, which by then she had regretted. She perfectly knew that she and Karl could not get married, but she still went along with it. She had difficulty resisting attractive men, despite the fact that, once she gave in to their advances, she felt pathetic. She had difficulty admitting to her aunt or anybody else that she enjoyed romantic relations with men. Her traditional upbringing forbade women from having lovers. Although she respected and valued her own culture, she still infringed its moral codes. She could not figure out the reason. Perhaps her life did not provide her with a sufficient sense of satisfaction, and she needed to fill the vacuum with some excitement.

As Mandana was thinking, Sima broke the silence:

"Mandana, do you have friends in France?"

Mandana thought for a few seconds, and said,

"Yes...why?"

"What kind of friends are they?" asked Sima. *"Are they close friends in whom you could confide, and who care for you, or are they simply people with whom you occasionally dine, drink, and go out to dance clubs?"*

Mandana understood Sima's point. For what Sima was getting at was her suspicion that Mandana lacked genuine friendships. By looking at Mandana she saw a young woman who sought to escape her empty life by travelling afar. Most of the girls she knew were always running after men, and when they found one they disappeared until their relation was over. Her own behaviour was not much different. Mandana's silence signalled to her aunt that she was probably right in her suspicion that Mandana had nobody in France. Sima would have liked to ask Mandana whether she had any hobbies, but Mandana's deep silence conveyed to her that further questions would not be constructive.

"Mandana, I believe we discussed this matter earlier when you arrived, but I think we have identified the root of your problem. You gave up your studies too soon, you did not invest in any true friendships, and you have no hobbies. You are basically filling your time with worthless momentary excitements cavorting with men, for you don't have any goals in your life. Because you know that you haven't achieved anything, you lack self-confidence. Most successful men wouldn't consider marrying someone like you."

"I agree with you on many points. However, life isn't that simple – that we follow the right formula and that all the blessings fall upon us – as your judgmental narrow mind seems to think. I know so many cases which would prove your neat little theory wrong. I know many women who have no skills, no money, no looks

— no prospects - and have ended up with wealthy young professional men. And I can see my own aunt, who is also young, warm and successful, but single despite her desire to get married as well."

"The women you are talking about did not sleep with men aimlessly. They were very focused in their strategy. They dated men as if they were following a university course. Their mothers, sisters and neighbours had been their teachers. We Oriental women had no examples to follow. Our mothers, aunts and cousins had hardly any experience in pursuing men. That is why I am single myself. However, I did something with my life as you mentioned. I became a successful business woman, not only thanks to hard work, but also thanks to one of the men I was hoping to marry. He did not marry me, but he gave me the opportunity to found my own business. As such I don't have any regrets. I am very proud of my achievements. I know that I didn't waste my life."

Mandana was not convinced by her aunt's display of self-satisfaction. Human beings can be so contradictory, she thought. The entire family knew that Sima was not a happy woman. Her failure at university had made her obsessed with academic achievement. Her failure to secure a handsome and successful husband had also left her rather bitter. Mandana did not have the impression that Sima was consoled by her own financial achievements. *"Perhaps she is in denial today,"* thought Mandana to herself. She knew that her aunt always came across as a very confident woman, but knowing her weaknesses she understood Sima better than those others who did not have these insights into Sima's intimate thoughts — she saw this self-confidence to be a façade. She did not envy Sima in any way, since she herself now owned a fortune of her own.

She decided to contain herself and not refer to any of her aunt's shortcomings. She turned to Sima instead and said:

"I am quite grateful for all the advice that you have given me since my arrival. I did not get the chance to share my plans with you, but I made up my mind two days before Jima passed away. I have decided to study fashion design in New York. I have always been interested in fashion and cosmetics and I am sure that I can start a great career in this field."

Sima went towards Mandana, hugged her and congratulated her:

Ganjbaran

"*I am proud of you. Don't ever let your life revolve around men or relatives. Human beings are generally very unreliable. If you meet the man of your life, if you find yourself in a city surrounded by your relatives, all the better, otherwise follow your own path and be focused. There is a greater chance that this way you will be happier.*"

THE NEW MYSTERY

The following morning, Azar and her family woke up before Sima and Mandana. Azar went to the kitchen to see what Chetra had prepared. Bahram and his sons went on the porch and saw Mona looking at the garden. Bahram noticed that Jima's corpse was no longer there. After he greeted Mona he went back inside and told Azar that Mona was on her feet and Jima's corpse had disappeared. The husband and wife did not know whether Mona knew about Jima's death. As they were debating what to do, their sons and Mona came in the kitchen. Azar went and hugged Mona, and asked her how she was feeling. Mona responded that she felt well despite everything that had happened. Bahram said that other women in her situation would not have been able to cope so well. Mona replied allegorically that children get lost everyday, but she was convinced that she would find hers.

"*Does that mean that you won't be leaving Ganjbaran until you find them?*" inquired Azar.

"*Yes,*" replied Mona.

"*What about your husband?*" asked Azar.

"*I don't know if I have a husband any longer,*" replied Mona.

While Azar and Mona were speaking, Chetra arrived with fresh *naans* she had made in the garden's tandoor. They all went to the breakfast room and were joined shortly after by Sima and Mandana. Bahram asked Sima discreetly if she had mentioned the news to Mona. Sima let him know that she had not. She then went towards Mona and took hold of her hand and said:

"*My dear Mona, you have been through a lot lately. However, I need to tell you something which might sadden you even more. But know that we are all here to support you.*"

"My children, Som, Kouros? Did they find their bodies?"

"No my dear," replied Sima, *"it's about your mother. She ... well she..."*

Some tears dropped from Mona's cheeks.

"I really don't know..." stammered Sima.

Mona interrupted her:

"Don't worry Sima, as you know well, my mother and I are not very close. Has something happened to her in Delhi while she was with you, Mandana?"

Mandana could not open her mouth to reply. Sima looked at Mona and revealed everything:

"Mona dear, your mother passed away yesterday."

Mona burst into tears, and Sima held her in her arms.

"I know she did not love me," repeated Mona trice.

Pedram and Rambod quickly finished their breakfast and left the room. Bahram followed them shortly after. Sima told Mona that she would be by her side for as long as she needed her:

"I know that you have been through a lot, but I know that you are a strong woman and that something positive will come up — there's a silver lining somewhere in all that misfortune."

The three women did not know whether Mona was listening or not. Mona turned and asked:

"Where is my mother's body? I want to see it."

"It's just here, outside, on the porch," said Sima.

"It was on the porch, but it has disappeared," said Azar uncomfortably.

"What do you mean, it has disappeared?" asked Mandana with a puzzled face. *"Who would want to steal a corpse? Jima's body was also too big for wild animals."*

"I can't believe all this," said Sima. *"Let's go on the porch."*

The four women arrived on the porch, and indeed there was no sign of any corpse.

"There isn't a trace of any wild animal coming here and taking her," remarked Azar.

"Why are you all blaming the disappearance of my children and mother on wild animals?" inquired Mona in an upset tone. *"All this doesn't make sense."*

"*Mona dear you are perfectly right,*" said Mandana. "*Too many strange things have been happening here.*"

"*Like what?*" asked Sima. "*Children and dead bodies disappear everyday. Are there other things that you would like to share with us? Is the brooch one of them?*"

"*You are really obsessed with that brooch,*" replied Mandana with a sly smile. "*Have you set your eyes on my jewels?*"

Azar interrupted the conversation before it could lead to a quarrel:

"*I think that we had better take care of Mona rather than argue about the specifics of the brooch. I know that we have failed to find Mona's children, and I am not certain that we would be able to find her mother's corpse either. As you know, my husband is planning to take my sons back to Canada. I feel guilty leaving you all behind. I am thinking of prolonging my trip a little in order to support you.*"

"*Thank you Azar,*" replied Sima. "*I am too overwhelmed by all these events which are distressing me. I shouldn't think about other things. I would love to have you stay longer, but it seems that Bahram wants you to go back with him.*"

"*We have all been through a lot in the past few days,*" reminded Mandana. "*Despite our little quarrel, I am not going to leave. I would be really selfish if after all these deaths and disappearances I left with the others. Also, I want to stay close to Mona and help her recover from the distress that recent events have caused her.*"

"*I am really overwhelmed by your thoughtfulness,*" said Mona. "*I had forgotten what it was to be part of a family. In London there was no one to care for me. I was so isolated. Now I understand how precious tightly knitted families are. I don't know what I would have done without you all.*"

A Postponed Departure

Azar felt obliged to stay as well. She thought that if the young hedonist Mandana had turned altruistic, she definitely could not pack and return to Canada. She felt that her presence would make a big difference to all three women. She went around the palace to find her husband and announce that she was not leaving.

Bahram was slightly irritated by his wife's decision as he was very dependent on her. Azar attended to his and their sons' needs slavishly. Whenever Azar was away, Bahram felt compelled to turn his flat into a military camp so that his home would remain in order. He would fill the kitchen with eggs and tinned food, and delegate like a general all the cleaning and washing chores to his sons. Seeing the miserable state in which Azar's relatives were, he felt too ashamed to impel his wife to leave.

In the afternoon Bahram succeeded in securing seats on a flight to Delhi for the following day. He also managed to book a flight back to Canada. His sons had enjoyed the past few days, as they thought that the search for Mona's children, the predictions of Bhaktijee, and Jima's death had turned their sojourn into an adventure. Nonetheless, they were happy that they were returning and thus would soon be able to recount their stories to their friends.

After helping her husband to pack, Azar went downstairs to speak to Mandana. She asked the young woman if she could consider settling in *Ganjbaran*.

"*Azar dear,*" said Mandana, "*to be honest I don't think I can even settle for good in a vibrant city like London or New York let alone Ganjbaran, where nothing is going on. However, I am not going to leave any time soon. I would feel guilty if I left in the coming weeks, but would get depressed if I stayed more than a month."*

In the afternoon, Mona went to take a nap, and Azar and Sima went for a walk. Bahram and his sons went hiking. Mandana stayed in the palace to organise her wardrobe, and was glad that Chetra had had no time to touch the items she had left behind. She told Chetra, however, that she was going to give her all of Jima's clothes once she had finished unpacking her belongings. She wanted to make sure that there were no gems or jewels left behind.

Once she had had enough of tidying, she went downstairs to eat a tangerine. As she was walking along the corridor, the phone rang. It was Karl calling from London.

HANDSOME BUT WORTHLESS

Karl wanted to speak to Mona. Mandana told him that she was asleep. Karl insisted that he needed to speak to his wife.

"*Your wife?*" scoffed Mandana, "*You must be joking? Mona has suffered a lot in the past few days, and you deserted her at the time she needed you most. By calling now and trying to show that you care for her, you are going to make things worse. Playing with people's feelings is evil. Just end the relation completely and let her wounds heal. It's clear to all of us that you don't love her. Why don't you just settle for a quick divorce?*"

Karl replied aggressively that he had no lessons to learn from Mandana, as she herself had had an affair with him. He reminded her if she really cared for her cousin, she would not have slept with him in the first place.

"*Thank you for reminding me of this,*" replied Mandana. "*I did realise that my act was morally wrong. But did you? Have you any conscience? In order to show people that you have some dignity left, please start divorce proceedings as soon as possible.*"

Karl replied that Mandana was being very harsh on him, and that getting a divorce was not that easy since there were financial implications. Their house in London was in Mona's name, and Mona had withdrawn nearly half a million pounds from their accounts. Mandana calmly asked Karl what his plans were. He replied that he was planning to file for divorce, but that he needed Mona to return his share of their wealth. Mandana then asked him to call later in the evening. But right before hanging up, she said:

"*Karl, you really are not worth more than an afternoon behind the bushes.*"

Mandana did not give Karl an opportunity to answer. She put down the receiver with the belief that it was incumbent on her to accelerate Mona's divorce. She knew that Mona was still in love with Karl, and that the process was going to be very painful for her. But Mandana believed the sooner the case was over the easier it would be for all of them. Mandana's main concern was the money in Jima's account. She did not want to reveal anything to Mona until her divorce case was settled. She was afraid that the news of a large inheritance might prompt Mona to make a stupid decision and stay with Karl. The major difficulty was to persuade Mona to give Karl whatever he demanded, so that the divorce would not be protracted.

A Message from Jima

S ome time around five in the afternoon, Mona woke up. Mandana did not get the chance to speak to her alone. Azar and Sima had arrived and wanted to see how she was feeling. Mona's face was rather pale but, at the same time, illuminated. Mandana looked at her and observed:

"It's as if you had seen a spirit, Mona."

"With all that has happened here," observed Azar, *"I wouldn't be surprised."*

"Many people in our family claim to have seen spirits," said Sima. *"But I have always been sceptical since I have never witnessed anything of the sort."*

Mona waited till she had everyone's attention and said:

"It might have been a ghost, my mother's ghost. I was asleep and she came to me in a dream. It was so real. She spoke to me and said that my children were safe. I asked her if they were with her, and she said no. She said that she did not want any children to follow her in the other world since she hated responsibilities. She advised me to divorce Karl as soon as possible. She said once he is out of my life the black cloud that has enveloped my horizon is going to dissipate and my children are going to be returned to me with bags of gold."

Mandana was so happy to hear Mona's dream. She felt a shiver and there were goosebumps across her arms as she truly believed that Jima had sought to communicate in metaphorical terms with Mona.

"Can you get a divorce from here?" asked Mandana excitedly.

"This wouldn't be desirable," interrupted Sima. *"She has to go to London as otherwise she might lose all her assets to Karl."*

"But do you think it's sensible to send Mona to London in this state for what may be a very stressful business?" said Azar.

"*I will accompany Mona as before,*" replied Sima, "*so that she will get all the necessary support.*"

"*Therefore, there is no point in me and Mandana staying here if you are all leaving for London,*" said Azar.

"*We could always accompany them to London,*" said Mandana. "*You could stay with us there until the case is finished and then go back to Canada. I will accompany Sima and Mona back to India.*"

Azar was very pleased with the new plan, as this allowed her to return to her family earlier and appease Bahram at the same time. She ran to announce the good news to Bahram. She then went to the kitchen to help prepare the dinner. Sima appeared shortly after to supervise Chetra. As they were opening cupboards and placing bowls and serving dishes on the table, Azar asked Sima when was she planning to book the tickets to London.

"*Before booking the tickets,*" replied Sima, "*I need to locate a legal advisor to save time. I have contacted everyone I know in London who could recommend a suitable solicitor. I don't trust people of this profession in general. Many of them are just a bunch of opportunists who want to make as much money as possible with the least effort possible. It's very difficult to find a committed lawyer who would actually assist you and not take you to the cleaners.*"

"*What makes you think that one of your contacts would know the right person?*" asked Azar.

"*I am just hoping. They have been living there for a couple of years; it might be that they have a solicitor as a friend. Otherwise we will have to find a solution ourselves.*"

Mandana had finally found a moment alone with Mona. She still did not want to disclose the existence of Jima's accounts. She was not sure if Mona had got over Karl. She wanted to encourage Mona to have more faith in her dream and the surreal so that she could overcome her difficult situation and not delay her divorce plans:

"*That dream of yours really gave me gooseflesh. Did Jima tell you anything else? She had such a strong faith in the gods. I wouldn't be surprised if they actually took her body and resurrected her in some way.*"

"*Mandana you are giving me the creeps,*" replied Mona. "*I know that my mother was fully devoted to the gods, but I would have difficulty believing that they have brought her back to life, after having put her to death.*"

"*I am not saying that your mother is now one of the living dead, but I think that they have taken her body away to bring back her spirit in a way that she would be of help to you. She might have seemed a bad mother when she was alive, but I can't believe that deep inside she did not have any affection for you. Our sanity is a very fragile thing, and it can easily be damaged by traumatic experiences. Jima was a victim of her poor fate and a captive of this sublunary world. Now that the gods have liberated her spirit, she can assume her maternal duties in the normal way.*"

"*In the normal way!*" exclaimed Mona.

"*I meant, like a normal person.*"

"*But she is dead!*" exclaimed again Mona.

"*Yes, but she came to your dream and spoke to you. This is extremely important,*" replied Mandana. "*Try to remember exactly what she told you.*"

Mona said, "*It's difficult to remember all the details now, but as I recounted earlier, she said that once Karl is out of my life, I will see my children with bags of gold.*"

Mandana jumped and hugged Mona, and said: "*There is only one way to find out that Jima is right, and that is to divorce Karl. The sooner you leave him the sooner you will see your children.*"

"*Are we not being a little superstitious?*" asked Mona.

"*Believe it, Mona.*" Mandana replied. "*Jima already had close ties with the gods when she was alive. I was even more sceptical than you are now, but so many extraordinary things have happened since I arrived in Ganjbaran. Whether it's the work of gods or the magic of Indian soil, I can't tell, but miracles definitely do happen here.*"

Forgotten Visas

Once again a travel fever spread all over *Ganjbaran*. Following two days debate about leaving or staying, at last everybody was packing. Some were excited, others not so. Mona was anxious. Sima was trying hard to find seats on the same flight as Bahram and his sons, but without success. Mandana was delighted by her aunt's inability to secure the flight, as it gave her the opportunity to show her deftness to her family. She called Maxime and managed to have all of them booked on the same flight to London.

There were, however, some technical problems that Mandana had not considered, namely, visas. She and Mona were the only ones with Western passports. When Bahram found out that Mandana had rerouted them via London instead of Zurich, he was about to explode. He and his sons were supposed to just transit through Switzerland; whereas now they were rerouted via the UK with no visas and supposed to spend two days in London. Mandana instead, of being thanked, was now blamed for having created further headaches for everyone.

"*You really need to consult people before taking any actions on their behalf,*" Sima scolded her niece.

Mandana resented being patronised and said:

"*Excuse me. You were trying to book flights yourself earlier and you failed. Could you please tell me how you managed to travel to Canada the first time without any visas?*"

"*I was planning to book flights via Turkey like the previous time so that we would get the opportunity to sort out our visas.*" replied Sima. "*Anyway, Bahram is the person who has been most affected by your meddling.*"

"*But I thought they had Canadian passports.*" said Mandana.

"*Not yet,*" said Bahram. "*But there is no need to argue over the issue. I am sure that Mandana can call back her contacts and rebook my original flight back to Canada.*"

Mandana called back Maxime, but was not able to recuperate Bahram's previous bookings. All the seats that week via Zurich were booked. He told Mandana that he could not find any flights which would allow Azar's family to avoid visas in Europe.

Such was Bahram's fury, he could have strangled Mandana. Everyone thought now that they were in limbo. They had packed without any travel prospects. Nobody wished to speak to Mandana, except Mona.

Mona turned to Mandana and said in a sarcastic tone:

"*It seems that my divorce is going to take a bit longer. Perhaps we should summon the gods and request their assistance.*"

It was as if Mona was vindicating, Jima who had been ridiculed by Mandana for the same reason. But as Mona finished her sentence the phone rang. Sima picked the receiver. It was Maxime. She called Mandana to the phone.

Mandana spoke for almost a quarter of an hour to Maxime. After her conversation she ran to Azar to announce that Maxime had solved their problem and that her family were to travel to Canada via Japan since the Japanese government did not require any visa from Iranian nationals. Sima, Mona and Mandana could travel via Istanbul, as no visa was required for Turkey either. Sima would then have a couple of days to sort out her visa to the UK.

Mandana went back to Mona and said:

"*I think you should consent to anything that Karl asks so that you could get your divorce on the spot. The gods are clearly doing their utmost to bring happiness to your life.*"

Mona needed badly to believe in the extraordinary, so she gave in. She and Mandana went to the garden and lit a fire under the arched structure beside the tandoor. They burnt wild rues and tangerine skins in order to appease the gods with the fragrant scents.

Two Generous Women

The following day, a small bus arrived to take all of *Ganjbaran*'s travellers to the airport. Bahram and his children were quite excited about the trip since they were having a two-day stopover in Japan before returning to Vancouver. Bahram was all the more pleased since he did not have to pay anything extra for the rerouting and his family's stay at the hotel in Tokyo. He did not know that Mandana had paid for his family's trip out of her own pocket. The young woman was keen for members of her family not to have any grievances against her. She knew that she had more money than she could ever spend on herself and therefore thought it was worth spending it on this occasion to avoid a family drama. Although she wished her family knew how generous she had been towards them, she could not tell them, lest they become suspicious of the source of her money.

Sima was expecting to be handed a bill in New Delhi, but was not much concerned about the expenses. She was a generous woman and believed that she earned enough to be able to take care of her family. Since Mandana was dependent on her father for money until her sojourn in *Ganjbaran*, it did not cross anyone's mind that Mandana had spent a rupee on their tickets. As a result, all the credit was given to Sima, and she was thanked profusely.

Both Sima and Mandana were looking forward to their trip to Istanbul. They were planning to enjoy boat rides on the Bosphorus and spend late afternoons in the cafés of Cihangir. Mona, on the other hand, was not too happy about leaving *Ganjbaran*. She was afraid that during her absence her children would show up at the palace and think that their mother had deserted them. She sat on the bus with a heavy heart. Mandana sat beside her, hoping to distract her cousin.

One by one, the members of the family boarded the bus. Right after the driver started the engine, Chetra came outside to wave farewell. Suddenly Mona opened the window and called Chetra saying:

"*If at any point you see my children, tell them that I am going to be back soon.*"

All the family felt really sorry for Mona. Mandana caressed Mona's back. Sima turned to her and said:

"*Mona dear, we will be back very soon.*"

And the bus went on its way to the airport.

A Survey of Love

Two weeks later, a black car drove to *Ganjbaran*. Sima and her nieces had returned. Chetra came to greet them. Mona told her family that she was extremely tired and had to lie down right away. Sima and Mandana, on the other hand, felt dehydrated, and wished to have tea together. They headed towards the drawing room, leaving Chetra in charge of the driver who was expected to carry the suitcases. After the driver left, the loyal servant went to make tea for the mistress of the house.

While Sima and Mandana were waiting for their tea, Sima turned to her niece and said:

"I am really proud of you, Mandana. Since your initial arrival in Ganjbaran, you have come to develop and improve into this fuller, better person – you've changed dramatically. You first appeared as a spoilt selfish puerile woman, thinking only of men and cosmetics. You seemed to have no aims in your life other than finding a husband. And now look at yourself! You have become a mature, caring woman, organising trips for your family and looking after your cousin. You are even planning to continue your education. I am all the more proud as I believe that I have been a positive influence on you."

Mandana did not know what to say in response – she certainly didn't think any change or improvement could be attributed to Sima. She was more convinced that it was rather the actual circumstances that had catalysed whatever change – the spectacular and dramatic events at *Ganjbaran* that seemed to have made her become in certain ways more mature. If Sima had said such a thing six weeks earlier, Mandana would have contradicted her and would have ended up bickering with Sima. But now she just replied:

"Of course, aunty, you have been my source of inspiration."

174

Sima felt that there was a tinge of sarcasm in that sentence, particularly in the word "aunty". At the same time, Sima was conscious that she had not invested much time in Mandana:

"*Mona also has been quite brave during the last few weeks,*" added Sima. "*I would like to believe that she has been following my example, but I believe that this has been more the effect of Bhaktijee's potions.*"

"*I totally agree,*" concurred Mandana. "*Divorce isn't an easy thing, especially if you are still in love with the other person.*"

"*Would you say that Mona is still in love with Karl after all that he did to her? I don't think any sensible woman would have wanted to stay with him,*" speculated Sima.

"*That is why she left him, because she was sensible, but nonetheless I could see that she is still in love with him,*" admitted Mandana.

"*This really doesn't make sense to me,*" protested Sima.

"*It shouldn't,*" said Mandana, as if she were a sage. "*It shouldn't. Love isn't a rational feeling. Haven't you been in love before?*"

"*Of course I have.*"

"*With a man who did not reciprocate your love?*" continued Mandana.

"*No, never,*" answered Sima.

"*Well, if you can't tell the truth, you might as well not see the facts.*"

"*I see. You seem to know something about my love stories. Jima probably spilt the beans before she died.*"

Mandana did not reply. She only looked at her aunt with fixed eyes, until Sima gave in:

"*Alright, I have also loved men who did not love me back. But I sincerely couldn't leave them.*"

"*But you had to...*"

"*Yes,*" uttered Sima, "*but Mona did not. She was married for several years. She could have delayed the divorce process, and tried to win Karl back. She did not put in any effort.*"

"*She did not put any effort, because there was no point in doing so. Your palace has not had positive effects only on me, but on Mona as well. It seems that by being surrounded by the idyllic surroundings of Kashmir, we have been able to reconnect with some divine forces which have released us from the grip of our emotional*" *dependence on other human beings. Look at yourself! You came to this place all alone, and yet you were extremely happy. Mona realised that she had the force to live on her own, without having to bear the miserable company of a man who did not love her. There was no point in staying with Karl. She chose to leave him while she still had some positive memories of her time with Karl."*

Sima was so impressed by Mandana's incisive insight that her jaws had literally dropped.

"This palace has undeniably extraordinary powers," said Sima. *"I should probably open an Ashram and help people rediscover their new talents. Yet I don't fully agree with you. I believe that the family support we provided also helped her break away. We proved to her that she wouldn't be alone."*

"There is probably a combination of factors that came into play. I think we should give Mona some credit as well."

Enchanted by Mandana's sudden oratory and display of wisdom, Sima perceived her now as an authority in psychology. She then confessed:

"I remember how in the past I crawled in front of these men so that they would marry me. I believed that in love one should put one's pride aside or else it would never materialise. Sometimes I humbled myself too much for men who were not worth my while. Perhaps the newer generation is wiser."

"There is no harm in going after the person we love, provided the other person is worth loving and has some affection for us. I have not met the men you dated, and therefore can't judge the situation; however, I have seen Karl. It was quite clear that he did not care about Mona. He left her at the worse moment of her life. He even gave up the search for his sons too soon, on a pretext. I don't know if he is simply heartless or if he had suddenly developed some aversion for his wife and wanted to free himself."

"I don't think there was much to understand in Karl's behaviour. First he goes all the way to Canada to collect his sons, and then he seems to take their disappearance as a blessing."

"In England, he felt humiliated as Mona had deserted him without giving any explanation," said Mandana with authority. *"He obviously thought that he was too good for Mona and that she would never dare leave him. In India his ego was satisfied once again as he saw that Mona was still in love with him and wanted to*

return with him to London. The disappearance of the kids was just a pretext. He is a typical unstable man."

Sima thought for a few seconds and said:

"The moral of the story seems to be: never give yourself entirely to men. It seems that if they are not challenged, they get bored of you and leave you."

"I think this is true for both men and women. Generally, human beings don't appreciate things they have, they take them for granted. However, I am convinced that if someone is truly grounded and happy, even when the initial passion and excitement have dissipated, the relationship will endure. The three pillars of a strong relationship are affection, respect and trust. Basically, the ideal relationship is the one we have with our grandmother."

"Why did you pick grandmothers as an example? You hardly got to know yours."

"That is how I imagine my relationship with my grandmothers would have been," replied Mandana.

"And that is how you imagine your soul mate would be?" inquired Sima with a tinge of sarcasm.

"Emotionally, not physically. No need to make a riddle of my taste."

"Your taste might not appear puzzling to you, but finding that type of man would definitely be a conundrum," remarked Sima.

Mandana, the Heroine

Sima ended the conversation and went to the kitchen to see what was being prepared for dinner. It suddenly dawned on her that Mandana had not claimed any money for the flights she had booked for the family a few weeks ago. Since she knew that Mandana was hiding something from her, she decided to interrogate her at another opportunity.

Mandana went into the garden for a stroll. She could not believe how much she had missed *Ganjbaran* and its gardens. The days were now becoming shorter and therefore she did not want to linger too long under the trees – even more so given the unusual events that had recently been unfolding. The young woman walked slowly in the garden watching the colourful birds flying from the branches of the trees to the fountain sinks where they hydrated themselves. At that moment Mandana felt so blessed that she thought she could never leave *Ganjbaran* for the overcrowded streets of London or New York. Over there, she thought, people are dehumanised by the lack of space and nature. Life was so calm and pleasant in *Ganjbaran* that she felt it was too unreal to be everlasting. However, she knew that in a few days, once she was well settled in the palace she would be bored, and would yearn for new shores. For the time being, she had one more mission to fulfil and that maintained some level of excitement. Mona had officially been granted a divorce, and Mandana had yet to reveal to her the existence of her late mother's estate which she could rightfully claim. She wanted to find the right moment, when Sima could not hear them; perhaps somewhere in the distant fields where they had originally located the pit 'of plenty'.

Mandana suddenly realised that the sun was about to set and she was amidst trees and bushes. She turned around to return to the palace, when she heard from behind some noises in the shrubs that she believed was caused by living beings. She thought some wild animal would spring out at any moment and harm her. Mandana did not even look back. She screamed and began to run towards the palace.

While she was running she could hear two children's voices shouting "*aunty Mandana*". Mandana suddenly stopped. She turned and saw Mona's sons running towards her with torn and muddy clothes. She thought it was a mirage until Kouros - the younger one - jumped into her arms. The child was clinging firmly to Mandana's shoulder. Som hung to her legs. Mandana had tears in her eyes more from awe than happiness.

Mandana put Kouros on the ground and said:

"*Your mother has been worried stiff since you two disappeared. We all, save for your mother, thought that you had disappeared for good.*"

Both boys said to Mandana in an excited voice:

"*Look at what grandma has given us.*"

Mandana looked and saw each boy with a small white purse. She undid the strings of one of them and saw a handful of what she was certain were ancient gold coins. Instantly, she got gooseflesh. She remembered Mona's dream. She rushed the two boys to the palace.

As the children were very hungry, they kept up with Mandana's fast pace. Once they arrived near the palace, Mandana began calling Mona. The children followed Mandana's example and started calling their mother.

Mona was in a deep sleep, but the three voices had penetrated into her dream. She could see them running towards the palace, while her mother was floating above them with her long dress in the air. Mona suddenly woke up. She could still hear the voices. She paused for a minute to make sure she was not dreaming. She was not! She ran down the stairs to the veranda. Sima arrived behind her. Both women could not believe their eyes. Sima was so happy for Mona that she wanted to hug her. Mona slipped away from Sima's arms and ran towards her children. As she reached down the porch's stairs, Kouros jumped into her arms. Som also wanted to hug her mother, but had to wait.

Mona began crying:

"*Thank you Mandana for finding my children. Thank you. I no longer need to take Bhaktijee's potions. I am cured!*"

"I think you should thank your mother. Look in the white purses," said Mandana.

Once Mona saw the gold coins, her body froze to the marrow. She looked into the sky to see if she could see her mother's silhouette, but did not see anything. She whispered:

"Thank you mother," and then said aloud, *"My mother did not hate me after all."*

She burst into tears once again. By then Sima had reached the garden as well and was hugging the children. Kouros asked why his mother was crying, and said that he was very hungry.

"Of course," said Sima. *"You poor babies, you must be starving. Follow me to the kitchen."*

Mandana stayed beside Mona, and caressed her hair as she was shedding tears. Mona sniffled:

"I couldn't believe all that has happened: Bhaktijee's power to see the future, my dream, the appearance of my children with purses of gold. It's as if the storm was over and I am walking over a bright rainbow."

Mandana dragged her a bit away from the palace and said:

"And you will keep on walking on this rainbow for many years to come. I am going to share a secret with you which you should keep to yourself and not question me too much."

Mona looked at Mandana with eyes wide open. She stopped crying and fully focused on her cousin's revelation.

Mandana did not want to mention anything about the prodigious pit and the jewellery. She turned around and disclosed:

"You are the happy heir to over seventeen million pounds."

Mona froze for a few seconds. Since everything that was happening was so extraordinary, she could believe anything she was told, however, fantastical. She believed Mandana without hesitation. She did not ask Mandana where the treasure had come from, she only said:

"I hope that all this isn't just a dream."

Mandana looked at her and assured:

"It's not. The only problem is that we might need to obtain a death certificate in order to get access to your mother's account. We should obtain one from the authorities here."

Mona was no longer listening to Mandana. Her mind was wondering away. She thought to herself that if the cost of losing Karl was to have her children return along with millions of pounds, then it was truly a fair bargain. So many men would now roll themselves at her feet. She paused for a minute and her smile vanished. She thought that she might end up completely alone, as she would no longer be able to trust any man approaching her. She believed that she was ugly and depressing and could not believe that any man would want her for her own sake. Any man who would chase her now, would be only for her money. She began crying again.

"*Why are you crying again?*" asked Mandana, tired of Mona's objections. "*It isn't going to be so difficult to obtain a death certificate.*"

Mona lamented:

"*An ugly rich woman with two sons would only attract parasites. I am going to end up alone.*"

"*I think we need to call Bhaktijee once again,*" said Mandana exasperated. "*He will do wonders for you.*"

"*What kind of wonders? Is he going to give me a facelift?*"

"*With the millions you have in your account you could easily have plastic surgery and change your figure. But is it really what you want? Look at me. Everybody thinks I am pretty. I also have millions in my account. Have I found the right man? No. Most men want to just sleep with me. It isn't worth changing yourself for anyone. And moreover, beauty is in the eye of the beholder. My mother thinks that Gary Cooper was handsome, but I think he was ugly.*"

"*Perhaps I shouldn't have left Karl,*" said Mona. "*Maybe I should return to him and tell him how much my accounts are worth. He may want me back.*"

"*This is the most idiotic thing I have heard in Ganjbaran,*" screeched Mandana. "*I waited all this time to reveal to you the existence of your wealth because I wanted your divorce case to be over and you wouldn't be tempted to say anything to Karl, and now you want to humiliate yourself by giving your money to him and be kicked out afterwards. The man isn't only mean and unstable, he also clearly doesn't love you any more.*"

"*This is impossible,*" cried Mona. "*He must still have some feelings for me. He is the one who came after me and asked for my hand...*"

"*Yes,*" interrupted Mandana, "*I am sure this is true. But that was years ago. People change. Then he was fascinated by you because you were different from the*" *women running after him – more peculiar. You got married soon after and he took you for granted as you waited on his hand and foot. If you treat someone like the epicentre of the Universe, then they believe that they can treat you as they please."*

"*What are we supposed to do then when we really love somebody?"* asked Mona. *"My mother worshipped all the gods in the world, and did not even care a bit about my father. Is that how I should treat my husband?"*

"*Your mother did not love your father,"* concurred Mandana with an air of understanding. *"It's true; however, your father worshipped her like his God. You seem to have turned out like your father. I am not advising you to become like your mother. Clearly she wasn't a happy woman, and I am sure Karl isn't a happy man either, otherwise he wouldn't have behaved as he did. In a relationship there shouldn't be any worshipping. You can worship the sun or a tree, but you can't worship a human being."*

Mona took a deep breath and remained silent. The two women returned to the palace and went into the drawing room. Mona picked a jug from a coffee table and poured water for herself and Mandana. She handed the glass to her cousin and groaned:

"*What am I supposed to do now? I seem to have hit the jackpot, but I am still unhappy. I don't know what to do with my life."*

"*The first thing you have to do is to change your attitude towards life,"* advised Mandana. *"You have two beautiful children; therefore, you don't have to fight against your biological clock like most unmarried women. You had a gorgeous husband, from whom you can keep fond memories. With age, he isn't going to keep his good looks, therefore you are not loosing much from that side either. You are now extremely rich, as such, you don't need a man to look after you. You had a mother who alive was worthless, but who, ironically, dead seems to be trying to look out for you and show you the affection she always denied you; therefore you have your own guardian angel yearned by us all. If you want to be unhappy and cry, that is your own business, but you virtually have no reasons to ever be sad again."*

As Mandana finished her sentence, Sima entered the room. She had heard Mandana's final sentence and said:

"*Mona might be unhappy, because she needs to be loved by a man."*
Sima did not know anything about Mona's newly acquired wealth. She could only identify Mona's situation with her own.

"*Men seem to be the very source of women's unhappiness,*" objected Mandana. "*The only women who seem to be happy with men are either those who are unscrupulous with them, or those who have found men who have women's soul.*"

"*You mean a transsexual!?*" exclaimed Mona.

"*Yes something of that kind,*" replied Mandana.

"*I wish I were a man,*" sighed Mona.

"*And I wish I were Indira Gandhi and governing India!*" exclaimed Sima. "*What is all this 'I wish I had', 'I wish I were'? Your sons have just been found. You should be over the moon.*"

"*Oh yes. Over the moon and the sun,*" chanted Mandana. "*You are hopeless Mona.*" Then she turned to Sima and continued, "*I am not quite giving up on Mona. I am going to take her with me on a quick trip to Delhi, and then my mission would be accomplished.*"

"*To New Delhi? What for?*" asked Sima.

"*I need to show her how the majority of the Indians live, and how grateful and resilient they are,*" replied Mandana.

"*No, that is going to be too depressing,*" complained Mona.

"*You already sound like a depressed woman anyway,*" observed Mandana, "*so the sight of poverty can't harm you; however, it might help to cure you from your depression; therefore we have nothing to loose.*"

"*When are you planning to leave, and what are you planning to do with the children?*" asked Sima.

"*We are going to take the children with us,*" replied Mandana. "*I am going to call Maxime tonight, and I will let you know about the date of our journey.*"

As Sima opened her mouth to say something, the children barged in the room. Kouros jumped into his mother's arms, and Som went to get a hug from Sima.

"*Som and Kouros told me the most extraordinary story about their adventure in the forest,*" said Sima. "*Would you want to recount it once again to mummy and aunty Mandana?*"

"*Yes, tell us how you got lost,*" requested Mandana.

The children were delighted to have the attention of the grown ups.

Som recounted that he and his brother were playing in the garden till their eyes fell on a marmot. They decided to chase it, but it was too fast for them and they eventually lost it. They tried to find their way back, but ended going around in circles in the forest. Kouros got very anxious and began crying. When the sun began to set, Som said that he started to get anxious too. Kouros then interrupted him and said that his brother began crying as well. They were hearing noises all around them, and thought that a wild animal was going to attack them. Suddenly a blue antelope appeared in front of them. At the beginning they were both scared, but the antelope was quite gentle. It kneeled down so that Kouros could get on his back. Som said that the antelope took them to a little cave behind a fruitladen walnut tree. The antelope had her two calves with her, and soon the children, the calves, and the antelope found a way to communicate. In exchange for her hospitality the antelope asked the two brothers to break the walnuts open for them. Som said that he and Kouros would spend hours each day breaking walnuts with stones until the antelope was satisfied. After a while, the two boys started getting bored with their assignment and the antelope tried to find them other tasks, like searching for other types of nuts and fruits. Som recounted that each time they got lost, the antelope would miraculously appear and lead them back to the cave. One day, as they were gathering little berries from the bushes, a big grey leopard came out from behind the bushes. Som said that they were terrified. They could see the mother antelope from afar, but she herself was too scared to come close. The leopard took slow but firm steps towards the boys. It was smiling and smacking its lips with its tongue. Som said that suddenly he saw his grandmother land from the sky in front of them and slapped the leopard in such a way that the leopard hit his head against one of the trees and passed out. She then went towards the two boys and asked them to follow her. Som said that they were too scared to pass by the leopard, but Kouros had an urge to touch it. The leopard moved slightly as he felt Kouros, and Kouros jumped in his brother's arms from his fright. The two boys ran after their grandmother. The mother antelope came to take the boys back to her cave, but Jima waived it away, castigating it for being such an incompetent babysitter. The mother antelope was very hurt. She dropped her head low, but still followed the old lady and her grandchildren as if asking for forgiveness. After a few minutes Kouros asked his grandmother if he could kiss the antelope good-bye. Som recounted that he did not wait for his grandmother's approval and ran towards his temporary adoptive mother, and Kouros followed him. They hugged and bid farewell. The antelope put its head on both Som and Kouros' head, shed a few tears and pushed them with its head towards their grandmother.

Som said that as soon as their grandmother saw Mandana from afar, she gave them a small purse of coins each and told them to run towards the young woman. She told them that she had to attend an important reception and would come back soon.

Sima turned to the other women and asked:

"*Could you possibly believe this story?*"

"*Every single word of it,*" chorused the two other women.

"*If you tell this story to anyone else,*" grinned Sima, "*they would think you are insane. Had I not heard Bhaktijee's predictions and Mona's dream, and not seen the purses of gold coins I would have thought that this is all the imagination of a creative child. I think that tomorrow morning we should go for a walk in the forest and ask Som and Kouros to locate the antelope's home once again for us.*"

"*And what if we come across the grey leopard?*" asked Mona apprehensively.

"*Then Jima will come and slap him hard in the face once again,*" replied Sima.

"*I don't think that we should be tempting fate,*" cautioned Mandana, sounding like an ancient oracle. "*I am certain that the antelope wouldn't want its life to be disturbed by adult humans. It doesn't expect to see Som and Kouros again as it has parted with them for good. Let the poor beast recover from its pain of separation and continue with its usual life. I am now going to go and make my call.*"

Mandana left the room, leaving Mona with Sima.

"*I can't believe that we have had such a conversation!*" exclaimed Sima. "*I am beginning to believe that the Thousand and One Nights is based on true stories.*"

"*Some Indian old lady told me in London that the Thousand and One Nights stories travelled from India to Iran,*" said Mona. "*Considering all that we experienced here, she seems to have been right.*"

"*I wonder if Jima is planning to haunt Ganjbaran or follow you on your trek?*" reflected Sima.

"*In our last trip to London, I hadn't the impression that she was following us; therefore, I believe that my mother has chosen to settle here.*"

"*I wonder if she left this world because of guilt.*"

"*What do you mean?*" queried Mona.

"*You don't need me to provide details my dear. Her attitude towards us and her words were neither particularly complimentary, nor friendly. But I shouldn't speak ill of a recently deceased.*"

"*Especially when they are haunting your palace,*" pointed out Mona.

Sima looked at Mona in a way that appeared to suggest that she had regretted her earlier comment, and in order to redeem herself added:

"*What happened in the past isn't really important now. Jima is now an angel, and that is all that counts.*"

Sima then changed the subject and asked:

"*Do you think I should come with you and Mandana to New Delhi?*"

As Mona knew that Mandana was taking her to her mother's bank and was not travelling to see beggars and vagabonds, she turned to Sima:

"*My dear aunt, are you now scared of being alone in Ganjbaran? I can assure you that my mother is going to look after you as her own beloved sister.*"

Sima felt that Mona did not really want her to join the trip. She said;

"*Never mind. Perhaps it isn't a very good idea anyway, as the trip to London was tiring enough and I should rest a bit while you are away.*"

Sima paused for a minute and continued:

"*I am going to contact Bhaktijee tomorrow and ask him about Jima. I am sure he will be able to communicate with her. She would be able to tell me what is the rationale behind all these incidents.*"

"*Why don't you ask me?*" suggested Mona. "*My mother might communicate with me tonight while I am asleep.*"

WHATEVER WILL BE, WILL BE

While Sima and Mona were conversing in the drawing room, Mandana had Maxime book her flights and hotels from Kashmir all the way to Kuwait for the following day. After her call she went directly to her room and packed a small suitcase and fell asleep.

The following morning she woke up before seven-o'clock and ran to wake up Mona. Mona had difficulty waking up, but since Mandana told her that they had a plane to catch, she dragged herself out of bed. Mandana asked Mona not to worry about her children and focus on getting ready.

Mandana took a quick shower, and in less than ten minutes she was ready and in the children's room. They were already up and playing with each other. Mandana took both boys to the bathroom, told them to undress and jump in the bath tub. She poured lukewarm water on them, without using any soap. She dried them, and sprinkled a large quantity of babypowder so that their bodies looked as white as a chalk. She then asked Som to dress, while she was clothing his younger brother. She then packed a small bag for them, putting a few clothes and toys, and went to inform Mona that she and her children were ready. Mona was still taking her shower.

Mandana usually needed forty minutes to apply her make-up, but it took her less than ten minutes to shower and dress up. Seeing that she had a couple of hours to kill, she went back to her room and sat in front of the mirror to apply her make-up. The children were getting restless and wanted to go and play in the garden. Worried that they would get lost once more, Mandana forbade them from going downstairs and gave them some of her make-up to play with and use on their face. By then Mona was ready and came to Mandana's room. She was taken aback when she saw her children applying make up and growled:

"*Oh my ... what on earth are you doing?*" Then she turned to Mandana and said, "*Are you trying to make transsexuals out of my sons?*"

Mandana laughed:

"*My dear cousin, you seem to be a little old-fashioned. Your sons are not going to turn into transsexual or homosexual simply by playing with make up once in their life time.*"

"*You never know,*" replied Mona. "*Anything that happens to people during their childhood has a very strong effect on them later in their life. Look at me, one of the reasons I am very shy and introverted is because my mother constantly criticised me and humiliated me for no reason. She never praised me.*"

"*I do understand,*" sympathised Mandana. "*There are experiences that do have a long lasting effect on children, but playing with a rabbit or make-up doesn't shape a child's sexuality or mentality. Don't think about who your children are going to sleep with when they are adults or what they are going to do with their lives when they are our age. Just enjoy them now while they are children. You did not decide to procreate in order to worry more, did you?*"

Mona did not know how to respond to what sounded to her as words of wisdom. She thought that her concerns were somewhat justified and contended:

"*You see my dear Mandana, I am now a single mother. My children have no longer a male figure in their life to look up to. I am scared that from now on, all their role models would be women, and this might have a strong impact on their sexuality.*"

"*How preposterous!*" exclaimed Mandana. "*Based on that logic, all boys bereft of a father necessarily grow up to be homosexuals.*"

"*Who knows Mandana, perhaps there is a link between the two.*"

Mandana realised that the conversation was leading nowhere. She herself held grudges against nature for creating men she could not seduce. She wanted all men to be attracted to beautiful women like her and not be distracted by members of their own sex. She also believed that there were too many handsome professional men being wasted dating other men and therefore generating a shortage of eligible men. She turned to Mona and suggested:

"*Mona dear, I can only advise you to send off your sons to play football and enrol them in martial arts classes. Then you can be assured that they will never turn out gay.*"

"*Would these activities compensate for the absence of a man at home?*"

"*Absolutely, provided you send them out every day to play with other boys. Not only you will be left in peace, you will also have one less thing to worry about.*" As Mandana finished uttering her sentence with her newly acquired tone of expertise, a little smile of satisfaction appeared on her face. She thought to herself that when people are worrying for stupid reasons, it's better to invent something to give them a peace of mind rather than reason with them.

Assured that her cousin was consoled, Mandana got up and announced:

"*We have to have our breakfast quickly before the car arrives. If you are ready, Mona, let's go downstairs.*"

A Moment of Melancholia

M ona and Mandana left in the morning, and once again Sima was alone in her palace. There were a number of pieces of furniture and windows which needed to be fixed, but she had not bothered to deal with them as she had preferred to spend time with her guests rather than supervise a worker from the village. She also had a huge amount of financial and legal paperwork sent to her by her accountants and lawyers that required her attention, but she had decided to ignore these till she was reminded again to sign them urgently. Now she had two days ahead of her to read them in detail.

She went to a room she had dedicated to her paperwork, but after ten minutes looking at her palace's deeds, she got bored and decided to procrastinate. She went out for a walk. She looked at the trees, the birds and the sky and ended up reflecting on some past events in her life. She thought about the last love of her life, who despite refusing to marry her, did not simply dump her and leave, but made sure his father gave her a job. Whenever he visited his father's factory, he went to check on Sima as well. He wanted to remain in touch with Sima, but once Sima left the soap factory, she did not see any point in seeing him. Deep inside she was unable to forgive him for marrying another woman. He had split with her without giving any clear reasons, just arguing that they were incompatible. Sima had no courage to insist for further explanations, as she was afraid it would hurt her ego. She was also not convinced that her ex-lovers' explanations would be useful, as their love appeared and disappeared like a virus.

She once told her mother that she envied women of previous generations, as they did not have to look for husbands. They were easily matchmade. Men did not have much choice but to marry, as they could not easily date women.

Her mother had replied that people always think that in the past life was better and easier. She said that matchmaking was not always ideal, as many women ended marrying men they did not love, and because women were not independent, they had to put up with the whims of their husbands. Sima saw that her mother had a point. She and her siblings, including Jima, had faith in their mother. She was a wise and capable woman, although her preference for her sons sometimes made her act unfairly towards her daughters.

Sima suddenly burst into tears. She missed her mother who had passed away only a year before her coming to India. She would give anything to have her back. She believed that her mother would have enjoyed living in *Ganjbaran*, as it had so many similarities to Iranian palaces.

A strong chilly wind blew from the peaks of the Himalayas and prompted Sima to return to the palace. It was shortly past noon. She did not feel very hungry and had a small tomato and cucumber salad with shallots. She then went in the drawing room and lied down. After a few seconds she fell into a deep sleep.

Late in the afternoon Sima was woken up by the ring of the telephone. Chetra had gone to answer, as it had been ringing for a while. Sima was frozen on the sofa, as she had a strange dream, where Jima and Bhaktijee were having a fight. In her dream, Jima accused the healer of cheating her family three times.

Chetra came into the drawing room and announced that Sima's sister Atoossa was on the phone. Atoossa sounded quite dejected. She had found out that Jima had passed away through a friend who had some vague connections with Karl. She asked Sima why she had not called her to let her know. Sima replied that she did not have her contact details. Sima added that she was hoping to get them from other relatives, but then got entangled with other urgent matters. Atoossa said that she felt very sorry for Mona, as she had lost her mother, husband and children. She thought that her niece had been cursed, and then began to cry on the phone. A smile appeared on Sima's face, as she announced to Atoossa that Mona's children had been found. She then mentioned the miraculous disappearance of Jima and her interventions from the other world. Atoossa was dumbfounded. She said she had difficulty believing the story.

"*My sister,*" said Sima, "*if you want to experience the marvellous things that I have told you, you have to come to India. Just last night, Jima came to my dream and said to me that Mona was getting married soon again. Such prophecies have been ongoing in the palace. When this one materialises again, then I am sure that you will believe me.*"

Atoossa, who had previously had no desire to undertake a long journey to India, pondered on that prospect for a while. She was very much attracted to the idea of experiencing some magic. She asked Sima details of her location and obtained some travel advice.

"*But before I let you go,*" interrupted Sima, "*could you interpret something I dreamt last night? In my dream Jima accused someone three times of dishonesty. It isn't the accusation that troubles me that much. It's the number of times the accusation occurred. Does this mean anything in particular?*"

Atoossa thought for a minute and told Sima to be content, and surmised that by repeating the accusations Jima was earnestly protecting her family from bad spirits. Thus, she ended the conversation with Sima on a happy note.

After Atoossa's call, Sima's melancholy also dissipated, she was fully restored, and famished. She went to the kitchen and asked Chetra to prepare her some sweet Kashmiri dish with raisins, but asked her to omit the chillies. She took four tangerines from the refrigerator, and went to her office. She spent an entire hour going through her various papers, and then returned to the kitchen.

BEAUTY GENERATES BAD LUCK

A couple of days later, as promised, Mandana returned to the palace but this time alone. Sima asked her what had happened to Mona and her children.

Mandana responded with an irritated voice:

"*Sima, sometimes I wonder if the gods' brains work normally.*"

"*If their brains functioned normally then they wouldn't be gods,*" observed Sima. "*But go on.*"

"*Mona is one of the most negative and ungrateful people on earth, and yet the gods provide for her always the best.*"

"*Mandana dear,*" Sima interrupted, "*I think you are being unfair towards Mona. Remember what kind of a mother she had?*"

"*And Sima dear, remember what type of a father I had? My childhood wasn't much better than Mona's. My father separated me from my mother.*"

"*Listen Mandana, I am not going to hierarchise your and Mona's grievances. However, when a mother hates her child, this has terrible repercussions on that individual. Anyway, it seems that Mona has aroused your jealousy. Let me guess what has happened. A handsome and rich young man fell in love with her and asked for her hand.*"

Mandana looked at Sima aghast:

"*How did you find out? Did she call you?*"

"*No, Jima told me.*"

"*This Jima is now ruining all the surprises of our lives. I guess we don't need to do much now, we should just close our eyes and go to sleep and she will tell us what comes next.*"

"*Don't worry too much,*" consoled Sima. "*She did not give me all the details. She just said that Mona was getting married soon. The only disturbing part of my dream was Jima's fight with Bhaktijee. I don't know how to interpret this. Atoossa believes that Jima by fighting against Bhaktijee is protecting us. However, it doesn't make sense to me. I don't think Bhaktijee is a bad man.*"

"*Perhaps he is,*" cautioned Mandana. "*You don't know everything about him, do you?*"

"*Never mind my dream - tell me exactly what has happened. I am intrigued to know how Mona found a wealthy husband amidst the slums of New Delhi.*"

Mandana had been so upset with her own fate that she had forgotten she had told Sima they were going to visit Delhi. Therefore, she told Sima the true story by substituting Kuwait city with Delhi. She cleared her voice and said:

"*It did not happen in the slum, but during a camel ride session.*"

Sima was a bit puzzled:

"*Camel ride in Delhi? Are you sure you were not in Rajasthan?*"

Mandana continued with the deceit and sneered:

"*It felt more like an Arabian desert. As Mona fell off the camel, an Arab prince dashed to her rescue. Mona had no injuries, but seemed to be slightly traumatised by the fall. I got off my camel and went forward to help her, but the Arab prince told me to let him take care of her. He opened a small tin and offered Mona some kind of candy. Mona took one and said that she would never ride a camel ever again. The prince laughed and asked us to have lunch with him so that he could have the opportunity to change her mind. Som and Kouros were still riding a camel, and were not paying much heed to us. The Arab prince asked me, if they were my children. I wonder why he did not associate them with Mona. He was a bit disappointed when I told him they belonged to Mona. At the beginning I really thought that he was interested in me, but during the lunch, it became clear that he had his heart set on Mona. Mona wasn't even smiling and looked even a bit aloof, while I was holding the conversation trying to enliven the table. My presence was quite useful to both of them. Since Mona wasn't willing to talk, the prince got all the information he wanted about her from me. When we parted and returned to our rooms, I was troubled by the fact that a man preferred Mona to me. Here I was, a beautiful single woman, warm and entertaining, and there was Mona, plain and cold with two kids. Shortly after our arrival, Mona knocked at my door.*"

She was standing at my door with a big smile, and a big jewellery box. She came in and opened the box. I couldn't believe what I was seeing in front of my eyes. I recognised the piece of jewel …"

Mandana suddenly stammered. She realised she was making a blunder. The piece of jewellery sent by the prince to Mona was a dark emerald necklace she and Jima had found in the pit. Mandana had recognised its heavy and large circle closures and the little diamonds surrounding the emerald stones. It was the exact piece of jewellery Jima had reluctantly sold in Kuwait.

As Mandana had paused, Sima asked:

"Was this piece of jewellery a part of the Iranian crown jewels?"

Mandana ignored the question and continued:

"The prince had sent a note along with the necklace, inviting both of us to dinner. Mona said she was worried as she did not know if the prince's intentions were honourable. I told Mona, honourable or not, his intentions did not really matter for he was young and handsome. Since she had not been with any other man except Karl, I told her to have a bath with rosewater and prepare herself for a night of excitement. She was appalled by my recommendation. She told me that she respected her body too much to give it randomly to any man who offered her a necklace. She said she would only sleep with a man who loved her enough to marry her. I responded that she is depriving herself of the pleasures of life by thinking that way. I reminded her that Karl married her, but then neglected her and fooled around with other women anyway. Marriage doesn't guarantee that you own the man."

Mandana stopped there and said she craved tangerines:

"I don't know how I am going to live without these Indian tangerines once I leave. Already two days without them was difficult."

"Weren't there any tangerines in Delhi? You left the country, didn't you?"

Sima was a master in lying herself, and now she was convinced that Mandana's story was half made-up.

Mandana did not reply to Sima's question.

"Why make such a mystery of your trip?" asked Sima. *"You are upsetting me now Mandana."*

Mandana thought that if she divulged the truth at this point, Sima would be even more upset. She thought it was too late to mention the treasure pit, and it was too difficult to build a new story. She stuck to her story once again:

"I am not making a mystery out of anything. Mona's second marriage is the only mystery here. If you don't believe me, wait till she gets in touch with you. I am sure that at some point she is going to get depressed and will want to visit you here in Ganjbaran."

"I hope for her own sake that she is going to get in touch soon, as I would throw her out of my palace otherwise for disappearing like this without thanking me and bidding me farewell. Now, you did not tell me how the prince proposed to her."

"Nothing extraordinary happened that evening. Both Mona and I went and purchased some fancy dresses for ourselves and the children, and went to dine with the prince."

This time Mandana was careful not to mention that they dined at the prince's palace. She then continued:

"During the dinner the prince said he would have waited to see the parents of her future bride before proposing, but since Mona had lost both of them he doesn't see any reason to postpone the matter. He offered Mona a ring with a massive diamond and asked her to marry him."

Sima laughed and said:

"You see Mandana, it's ironic that you gave Mona so much advice about a number of matters, but in the end, she knows better than you how to bag a husband. She lets herself be desired and lets the man understand with her words and body language that he couldn't have her unless he commits himself. Whereas you, when you fancy a man, you give yourself right away."

"You may be right," conceded Mandana in an irritated tone, *"but, nonetheless, what I don't understand is how a man who can have so many other women at his feet could go for a plain woman like Mona."*

"Mona is ugly in your eyes, but perhaps for him she looks like his mother or a beloved aunt. Appearance isn't the only criterion for attractiveness."

"Well, it certainly isn't in Mona's case," acknowledged Mandana. *"The uglier you are, the more good-looking wealthy men you get. However, Mona is neither the warmest person on earth... she hardly smiles, jokes, or talks."*

"It's her innocence that attracts these men, it seems. In a world where women appear desperate to get married, and are ready to roll themselves in the mud for them, a woman who exudes such indifference is refreshing."

"Just live and learn," sighed Mandana.

"*Yes, unfortunately you never live long enough to learn. That said, finding a man shouldn't be your ultimate goal. A life partner should be a means for achieving your goals.*"

"*What do you mean?*" asked Mandana.

"*Remember when Mona was married to Karl? How many tears did she shed? If her goal was to achieve happiness, then she definitely missed it.*"

"*But Mona is an unhappy woman. Whoever she marries she will be unhappy.*"

"*Then why do you envy her?*" inquired Sima. "*The poor woman might end up sharing her palace with three other wives of the Sheikh, and who knows how many mistresses.*"

"*I don't envy Mona and her marriage to the Arab prince, as you say. I am just upset because I know I am prettier and wittier than Mona, yet in this case, not as popular with men as her. When a man prefers another woman to me, it makes me insecure. I wonder what I did wrong. For weeks I question myself.*"

"*Well you shouldn't,*" advised Sima. "*Every person has a different taste. If you think that way, you can't criticise Mona for being an unhappy woman, as clearly you are not going to be a happy person either. During your life time you are going to experience many other occasions when men would choose other women over you, and, as you grow older, this is going to be ever more recurrent. What are you going to do when you reach fifty? From now on, your attitude should change. You should be happy that Mona found a handsome wealthy husband, especially because she is dull in looks and personality, and has two kids which would probably put off many men. This occurrence should prove that there is hope for every single one of us.*"

"*I guess you are right,*" conceded Mandana once again.

"*Had you really taken Mona to one of the slums of Delhi, you would have been more appreciative of what you do have. Don't forget that very recently you had a man dying to marry you and another one wooing you in Delhi. It was evident to me that even Karl had a soft spot for you. Azar was constantly asking me whether you and Karl were having an affair.*"

Sima paused for a short while and then asked once again:

"*So Mandana, tell me where did you travel with Mona?*"

Mandana looked at Sima with a composed smile and replied:

"*Delhi, but not the slum.*"

"*I never got to ask you how you managed to pay for everyone's tickets to Japan and Turkey. I doubt that your father would allow you to be so liberal with his money,*" commented Sima.

"*Hasn't Jima told you yet despite all her appearances in your dreams?*" scoffed Mandana. "*I sold the brooch and paid off the bills. Another person might have thanked me for my generosity, but you put me through an inquisition instead.*"

Mandana then left the room and headed towards the garden. Sima's interrogation had annoyed her and she decided once again that it was time for her to leave *Ganjbaran*. There was no point in staying any longer. Besides Jima's occasional appearances in their dreams, Mandana could not foresee anything of much significance happening any time soon. With Sima getting on her nerves, she thought it best to leave as soon as possible. As she was going down the stairs from the porch, she paused and went back up the stairs. She then ran towards the phone and dialled a number:

"*Good evening Maxime... I want to leave Ganjbaran tomorrow. I don't know why I came back. I need a ticket to Rome... I have another aunt there... yes, one ticket this time.*"

Tears of Lonliness

That evening, Sima ended up dining alone. She called Mandana, and even went to her room to see why she did not want to join her. She saw that Mandana had packed her suitcases and was lying on the bed. Mandana announced her departure and told her that her previous trip had exhausted her and that she needed some sleep.

While eating alone, Sima was suddenly overwhelmed by a profound sense of solitude – warm tears began to stream down her cheeks. With the saltiness of her tears lingering on her lips and tongue, Sima could not understand what was happening to her. She felt as if her heart had become heavier. She felt totally isolated, and thought that nobody really cared about her. She thought that all her relatives had taken advantage of her hospitality as if it were her duty to offer them room and board. She was tormented by the thought that she was simply a means to their ends, and that, really, they had not an iota of affection or concern for her wellbeing despite the lengths to which she had gone to help members of her family. Sima was reflective and intelligent enough to realise that it was these suspicions niggling her and bringing her down. She thought she should seek to dissect them to see whether they stood to reason. She reflected on how others benefited from her insights, but that ironically she herself was failing to console herself by them.

In search of the source of her grief, Sima concluded that it must have been her feeling of solitude that had brought her down. Seclusion was not a trait of her culture. Nobody in her family had ever spent a week alone. Nonetheless, after the revolution, she was yearning to move to a distant place, far from her relatives, for some peace and rest. She had enough of all the gossip and the social expectations. In India she was hoping to find some respite, but she had not taken the time to think if a life as a recluse suited her. However, in the last few months she did not even have time to think of her future, as her family dragged her into a series of mishaps. Now that she was given the opportunity to live all alone and enjoy her peace, she did not want it. What was she going to do after Mandana left, she thought? Would she have to look for a companion in order to abate her sense of loneliness? She thought that chasing men at her age was degrading, and a sign of despair. However, she did not want to be pointed to as a spinster. '*Is forty five too late to get married? Are suitable men still available at that age?*' Sima's mind was now restless. The thought of loneliness daunted her, and once again she burst into tears.

That night, when she finally went to bed, Sima realised that she had lost her sense of purpose. She had many plans initially which fizzled out after Jima and her nieces arrived in *Ganjbaran*. She decided that on the morrow, after Mandana's departure, she would pull herself together and take up some charity work in Kashmir. '*Who knows? Maybe I will meet interesting people somewhere down the line.*' With this positive note in her mind Sima fell asleep.

Departure is Always an Option

The following morning, Mandana got out of bed at seven-o-clock. She showered and dressed in less than ten minutes, and then spent forty minutes in front of the mirror applying make-up. This time Sima did not want to miss her niece's departure. She too got up early to have breakfast with her. Seeing that Mandana was not coming downstairs she went to get her.

Mandana's door was open and she could be seen applying some Iranian mascara on her eyelashes. Sima asked her who she was adorning herself for, and Mandana replied anyone who had an eye.

Sima laughed:

"Aren't you going to have some breakfast before you leave?"

Mandana picked her handbag and followed Sima downstairs. They headed towards the breakfast room, where fresh *naan* made by Chetra, cheese, butter, tea and cucumbers were waiting for them.

Sima still did not know Mandana's destination, so she asked:

"Are you going to the US?"

"No, I am going to Rome. I am planning to stay a few days with aunt Atoossa and her daughter."

"But after that. Aren't you going to go to the US to study design?" persisted Sima in a surprised tone. *"Does Atoossa's daughter at least know that you are visiting them?"*

"No, she doesn't. They will find out once I arrive there. I have asked Maxime to book me a hotel room in any event."

"And your US plans?" repeated Sima.

"I have changed my mind. I don't want to live in the US. Young people go there to work and earn money. I want to enjoy life. I am planning to study Italian, and who knows perhaps I will then go on to study art."

"You mean you want to settle in Italy!" exclaimed Sima.

"Yes, I want to stroll between the ancient monuments of Rome. And moreover, Italians are so similar to us. I don't think I will get homesick there. Didn't Mona meet her first husband in Rome as well?"

"You are incurable, Mandana. I had high hopes for you, and now I am afraid that you will indulge in idleness and ruin your life among the ruins of Italy."

"Is this yours or Jima's prediction?" asked Mandana.

"Its mine." replied Sima.

"Then I need not worry," said Mandana laughing. *"Perhaps you should come and settle in Rome as well. I can't possibly see you living here all by yourself."*

"I feel too much at home in India to leave, but I will think about it."

The two women heard a car arrive and left the table. Chetra went out and called the driver to help her carry Mandana's two suitcases to the car. Sima hugged Mandana and said:

"I truly enjoyed having you here Mandana. I will miss you. Come back soon."

"Thank you, Sima for your hospitality. I wil keep fond memories of Ganjbaran."

Mandana beamed as she uttered that sentence, as memories of her discovering the jewels with Jima, along her moment with Karl in the gardens of *Ganjbaran* behind the bushes came to her mind.

Sima accompanied Mandana to the car. They kissed and hugged each other once again, and the car drove away. Unwillingly, Sima burst into tears yet once more. All her family were now gone. Once she had relieved herself of the pain, she pulled herself together, dried her tears and reminded herself that the option to leave was always open to her.

While the car was still running in the driveway, Mandana turned around to take a last glimpse of *Ganjbaran*. As she looked at the palace, her smile disappeared and her eyes remained fixed on it. She kept on looking until the palace was no longer in sight.

WHY BOTHER CRYING?

At noon, Sima had a very light lunch; a coriander salad with tomatoes, and a small slice of cauliflower *koukou* (a Persian savoury cake). She then went to her office and searched for the maharajas' phone number. They had been quite resourceful when she bought *Ganjbaran*, therefore she believed they could connect her to well-placed people who could help her set up a charity. Once she found the contact numbers she realised that her office needed a telephone, but unfortunately the room had no socket. She thought that she should fix the problem, but wondered if there were any electricians in the vicinity. Grudgingly she went into the hallway to make her call. As she put her hand on the receiver, the phone rang. It was Atoossa.

Atoossa announced that she and her daughter, Mina, were planning to visit her.

"*You are leaving tomorrow!?*" exclaimed Sima, "*but Mandana is ... allo, allo, allo.*"

The connection was lost and Sima was not able to convey that Mandana was on her way to visit them in Italy. Sima tried to call Atoossa back, but her line was constantly busy. She decided to try later. She forgot then to call the maharajas, and only remembered once the phone rang again.

Sima thought it was Atoossa again, but this time it was Mona. Sima could hardly understand her as Mona was crying and panting. Sima asked her a few times what had happened, but Mona could hardly string a few words together. Towards the end of the conversation, she understood that Mona was going to return to *Ganjbaran*.

As her conversation with Mona ended, Sima said to herself that she was practically sure that Mandana would return as well, since she was not the type of person to stay by herself in Italy, unless she fortuitously met a man. She then wondered that now that her relatives were coming back, would she still feel the need to busy herself with demanding charity work in India? She thought about it the whole night until she exhausted her brain and fell asleep.

Between Scylla and Charybdis

The following morning, Sima woke up quite distraught. Jima had appeared in her dream and asked her to get in touch with Farshid before he passed away. It was not Farshid's death that troubled her so much, but more the fact that she was told to speak to him. Although any prophecy Jima had communicated through dreams had always materialised, she still did not want to believe what she had dreamt.

It was still early in the morning, and the sun was still working its way up the sky. Sima sat on her bed and spoke as if someone were in the room:

"*Jima, why must you annoy me with such a request? You of all people never gave a damn about anybody, and now you wish me to call Farshid? Answer me now as I am now finding your disjointed communications through our dreams quite annoying.*"

As Sima finished her sentence a huge bird dropping hit one of the two windows of her room. It was as if a big pre-historic bird had flown over Sima's palace. Sima wondered if this was indeed Jima's reply, and did not know what to make of it. She got upset and said:

"*And I thought that you had matured after your supposed death, and here you are acting like a deranged woman yet again.*"

Another huge bird dropping hit the other window.

Sima shook her shoulders and went to take a shower. In the middle of her shower the water turned extremely chilly. Nearly slipping in the bath-tub, she picked her towel and came out. She was convinced that Jima was upset at her and aiming to make her life miserable. She believed that she had two options, either to sell *Ganjbaran* or to call Bhaktijee to come and exorcise the place, and get her rid of Jima. Since she was scared that Jima would do something worse, she called Chetra and asked her to locate Bhaktijee.

Sima was about to leave the hallway when the telephone rang again. It was Mandana. She sounded quite upset, as she had arrived in Rome and could not get hold of Atoossa and her daughter. She had even travelled to their house, but even the housekeepers seemed to have left. Sima told her that after her departure Atoossa had called, and she was on her way to *Ganjbaran* with Mina. Mandana said that she was so disoriented that she needed to come back.

"*Of course, my dear. This is your own home,*" Sima told her niece.

Once she hung up, she saw Chetra waiting behind her.

"*Sorry, Chetra,*" apologiese Sima. "*I was not expecting antoher call. There is no need to call your cousin in the village to locate the Bhaktijee. I am ready to walk all the way there to fetch Bhaktijee myself. I can't wait, as the matter is urgent.*"

Two hours later, Sima and her loyal servant were back with Bhaktijee. Bhaktijee put his little bowl made out of a carved stone on a short pillar standing in the garden. He put some seeds and some sandalwood in the bowl, and began chanting incantations in an obscure language. Fifteen minutes into his chanting, the water in the basin began swirling fast. Sima was terrified. Bhaktijee had been chanting for nearly an hour when they all heard a scream followed by a deep silence. The water stopped swirling, and Bhaktijee stopped chanting. He told Chetra that Jima was now locked out of this world and would no longer trouble Sima; however, before leaving she might have cursed *Ganjbaran* by inviting some evil spirits to haunt it. If this were the case, it would be dangerous for Sima to spend even a single night there. Once Chetra translated Bhaktijee's words for her, Sima was panic-ridden. She decided to leave before sunset. She asked Chetra to call people from the village to come and help her pack up her belongings. She told Chetra that she should also call some men to come over and tidy up the gardens so that she could sell *Ganjbaran* in the coming weeks.

Bhaktijee, who understood Sima's plan, told Chetra to tell her mistress that her intentions to sell the place to another buyer were immoral, as the new buyer would be the victim of the spirits. Bhaktijee said that Sima might then be punished for her deed.

Sima was very disturbed by Bhaktijee's prediction. She looked at him and said that she had invested a fortune in *Ganjbaran* and could not just let the place fall into ruins. Chetra told Sima that Bhaktijee opines that sometimes we make wrong decisions and that, surely, she must appreciate that investments also carry risks.

Sima's heart started beating fast. She looked at Bhaktijee and Chetra and said she did not want to waste more time and wanted to start packing right away. She asked Bhaktijee what her options were, as she had difficulty abandoning the palace without getting any compensation for it.

Bhaktijee asked in a serious tone to be given the keys to the palace. He mentioned that he would see to the restoration of serenity in *Ganjbaran*. He added that he needed some time for this task and that Sima would need to be patient. Sima wondered how much time he needed, and Bhaktijee said that to get rid of evil powers might take many years.

Sima felt that Bhaktijee was trying to con her out of her property. She soon realised that in her efforts to get rid of one nuisance by getting Jima's spirit exorcised, she ended up with another nuisance in the shape of Bhaktijee. She regretted then that she had let Jima leave, as she was now dreading Bhaktijee and wished Jima could come and advise her. She thought she had been too hasty to judge Jima, and now she had to face the consequences. She did not say more to Bhaktijee except that she would be handing the keys to Chetra upon her departure. Bhaktijee then asked Sima to sign a deed allowing him to run the place during her absence so that he would not have any problems with the authorities. He asked Chetra when calling the village to invite the chief of the village to *Ganjbaran* as well, to act as witness.

By this time Sima had become quite annoyed with Bhaktijee. She decided to put him to sleep with the herbal sedatives he himself had left for Mona. She invited Bhaktijee in, and told Chetra to take care of the packing while she was going to prepare a meal for Bhaktijee. She did not trust Chetra as she knew that Bhaktijee was a revered figure in her village. She herself admired Bhaktijee before his exaggerated requests where unravelled to her. She took some cooked lentils from the refrigerator and prepared a coriander and tomato salad. She let the seeds that Bhaktijee had given to brew for five minutes and then mixed it with some Masala tea, over-sweetening it in order to hide the taste of the seeds, despite the fact that both the herb and the seeds were supposed to be insipid. She sprinkled the salad and the lentils with a few spoons of the herbs and took them to Bhaktijee, who by then was very hungry as it was an hour past noon.

Right after his meal Bhaktijee sat on a sofa in the reception hall and fell into a deep sleep. Sima was so satisfied with her achievement that she rotated once around herself and ran upstairs to pack. She reminded herself of what she had once learned from her mother, that the extent to which magicians are powerful depends on how much credence we offer them – basically, they yield as much power over our minds as we're prepared to concede to them.

Once the expected group of people arrived from the village she ushered them inside and asked Chetra to supervise their packing. She asked them to leave most of the furniture behind as they were already in the palace when she arrived and had no desire to take them. She also forbade anyone from waking up Bhaktijee. She sent the chief of the village back, saying that they were not going to make any transactions and apologised for the inconvenience.

While the villagers were busy packing Sima's belongings, Sima called her estate agent in Bombay and told them her plans. She asked them to find her a temporary flat in Colaba and send a van to *Ganjbaran* in order to pick her carpets, and crockery. She was appalled at the cost of renting property in Bombay and thought she was being swindled by the agent. No matter how much the agent swore that Bombay's properties were one of the most expensive in the world, Sima remained sceptical, but accepted at the end to pay the asking price as she would rather have one less thing on her mind; she needed a place to stay right away. She then called Mandana's friend Maxime, asking him to locate all her relatives travelling to India, emphasising Mandana's name. She wanted him to inform them that she would be leaving for Bombay in the coming 24 hours and therefore they should change their destination. She also asked him as sweetly as she could to organise her trip from *Ganjbaran* to Bombay.

THE EVER PRESENT SISTER

A fter her call, she went to her room to pack her valuables herself. Suddenly she was struck by fatigue. She shut the door and lay on the bed, hoping to close her eyes only for five minutes. As she fell asleep, Jima once again appeared in her dream.

"*I thought Bhaktijee had sent you away for good!*" exclaimed Sima.

"*Bhaktijee has no such powers,*" replied Jima. "*He is a kind of herbalist, not a warlock. He has realised that you are overestimating his powers and he is taking advantage of it. I am quite disappointed that you invited him to lock me out of this world when all I have done up to now is help all of you.*"

"*But you sent me huge bird droppings from the sky, and cut off hot water.*"

"*Don't be absurd. Geese and ducks have always defecated from the skies, and old houses have always had poor water pressure. All these have been just a coincidence. I have better things to do now than sending excrements. Once one becomes a wandering soul, wordly matters and human insults don't matter so much.*"

"*I am really dreading Bhaktijee now,*" said Sima. "*You tell me that he has no powers, but he was able to make the water of the pool swirl. I even heard an awesome scream from afar.*"

Jima began laughing:

"*My dear sister, I could have never imagined you to be so credulous. Bhaktijee could perfectly pay someone to hide behind the trees of your palace and scream. Your palace seems to be full of hidden devices of which Bhaktijee seems well aware. For instance, behind the pillars some five hundred meters from the pool, there is a small contraption that can make the water spin.*"

"*What does it look like?*" asked Sima.

"You will figure it out once you see it. I felt that you needed my help, and here I am to comfort you. I will take care of Bhaktijee. Go and sell your palace in peace. Enjoy your time with Atoossa in Bombay. Just don't forget my request to call Farshid before it's too late."

Suddenly Sima woke up, this time serene. She rushed downstairs, went into the garden and looked for the pillars. She ran towards them to look for the device. She discovered a spiral shaped carving protruding from the pillar. She twisted it and ran towards the pool to see if it had any effect. She could not believe her eyes, the water was indeed swirling. She went back, and twisted the device in the opposite direction and sent a kiss upwards into the sky to Jima. She then hurried back to her room to finish packing her suitcase and handbag.

She checked a couple of the guestrooms upstairs and saw that the bed sheets had been removed and only bedspreads were covering the mattresses. She then went downstairs to check on her temporary staff, and saw that they had all gathered sipping tea happily chatting away. Sima turned to Chetra and asked if they were done with their tasks. Before Chetra could answer her, the telephone rang once again. Maxime had called to confirm Sima's flight to Bombay, and informed her that a car would be picking her up the following day at two in the afternoon.

As Sima turned around to leave the hallway, Chetra came to her slightly concerned that Bhaktijee had been sleeping for too long. Sima told her not to worry as Bhaktijee was in a deep meditation trying to ward off the evil spirits. She then asked Chetra if the list of items she wanted packed were stored safely in the drawing room and if all the used rooms of the palace were tidied as she expected. Chetra confirmed that indeed they were, and they both went through the rooms to see if anything had been forgotten. Chetra then turned to Sima and asked in a disturbed tone whether she was going to dismiss her soon. Sima gave her the option to accompany her to Bombay or to receive six months' pay and leave. Chetra did not like either option as she needed a job and at the same time did not want to be far away from her family. She asked whether Sima was not planning to leave the palace in Bhaktijee's custody and therefore allow her to look after the palace with him. Sima told Chetra not to worry too much. She assured her servant that, she would recommend her to the new owners without any reservations. She ended by telling Chetra that during the lunch Bhaktijee had changed his mind and that he was no longer interested in remaining in the palace.

Sima prevented Chetra from pursuing the conversation further, and asked her to call the villagers so that she could pay them for their work.

After the villagers received their wages, Sima asked them to take one of the mattresses and put it on a slab of wood and carry Bhaktijee back to the village. Once they left with Bhaktijee, she turned to Chetra, who was watching the crowd leave, and asked her to reconsider her offer to remain in her service in Bombay and advised her to answer in the morning. Chetra told Sima that she will think about her offer but would be grateful if Sima could pay her wages straight away, as she wanted to leave while her fellow villagers were still in the vicinity.

Chetra took her money and a large bag filled with Mandana's unwanted items and left. An hour later, a heavy shower poured on *Ganjbaran* followed by a thunder storm. Sima went through all the rooms to make sure that the windows were closed. Ironically, the rain storm was giving her a sense of security as she felt that in such weather no unwelcome being would venture towards *Ganjbaran*.

Now that she knew she was leaving *Ganjbaran* for good, she started admiring once again the grand domed hall of her palace with its stained glass ceiling. Her eyes fell on a large old radio standing under a painting. She turned it on without much hope that it would produce any sound. A sweet Indian melody of tabla, zither and bansuri flute flowed like a lullaby from the magic box and put Sima to sleep.

TIME TO LOCK THE GATES

The following morning, Sima woke up before dawn. The radio was still on, emitting abrasive sounds. Sima was bundled in her pashmina shawl. She turned the radio off, and heard the singing of Kashmiri flycatcher birds. She went upstairs to take her shower and get ready for her final walk in the ever green gardens of *Ganjbaran*.

Before going out, Sima put on a cashmere sweater and wrapped a wide shahtoosh shawl around her neck and shoulders. She took a big apple and headed towards the garden. She stepped slowly down the stairs biting into the fruit, and went across the pools into the fields. The weather was quite cold and the plants were covered with dew. Sima held on tightly to the shawl. She felt mildly anxious and had butterflies in her stomach. The previous night she had been thinking she would be sad to leave *Ganjbaran*, but that morning she could not help smiling. She still felt a bond between herself and *Ganjbaran*, but this was similar to her ties with Iran. If she could leave her country and her endless memories, she could leave her idyllic paradise-like palace too. In addition, Bombay was a buzzing city and a dramatic change from the quiet life at *Ganjbaran*. Moreover, all her family was bound to join her once again, although she did not know whether the crowds and beggars of the megalopolis were not going to scare some of them away. She looked upwards to the sky where the sun was hidden behind a few clouds and said:

"*Jima, I bet you will be staying here. This is the place where we should all gather once we have left the flesh of our bodies.*"

Sima thought Jima would respond by some means, but nothing happened. Her gaze fell upon a few wild flowers which seemed to relish the cold weather.

212

Her smile widened as she thought that if she were a flower, she would be the resolute geranium which could grow anywhere.

Early in the afternoon, the car Sima was expecting, arrived. On her way out, she asked the driver to stop at the main entrance of *Ganjbaran*, and help her close and lock the heavy gates. As the car drove away, she did not turn to look back. Instead, she took from her bag a magazine with images of Bombay and browsed cheerfully through its pages.

15830855R00124

Made in the USA
San Bernardino, CA
22 December 2018